The Exception

Sandi Lynn

Sandi Lynn

The Exception

Copyright © 2016 Sandi Lynn Romance, LLC

Photo & Cover Design by: Sara Eirew @ Sara Eirew Photography

Models: Mat Wolf & Sheina Loubier

Editing by B.Z. Hercules

Books by Sandi Lynn

If you haven't already done so, please check out my other books. They are filled with heartwarming love stories, some with millionaires, and some with just regular everyday people who find love when they least expect it.

Millionaires:
The Forever Series (Forever Black, Forever You, Forever Us, Being Julia, Collin, A Forever Christmas, A Forever Family)
Love, Lust & A Millionaire (Wyatt Brothers, Book 1)
Love, Lust & Liam (Wyatt Brothers, Book 2)
His Proposed Deal
Lie Next To Me (A Millionaire's Love, Book 1)
When I Lie with You (A Millionaire's Love, Book 2)
A Love Called Simon
Then You Happened
The Seduction of Alex Parker
Something About Lorelei
One Night In London
Second Chance Love:
Remembering You
She Writes Love
Love In Between (Love Series, Book 1)
The Upside of Love (Love Series, Book 2)
Sports:
Lightning

Table of Contents

Chapter One
Jillian

I could hear the soft music play as the guests started to gather inside the church and took their seats in the wooden pews that were beautifully decorated with white satin bows and white roses. My mother and my bridesmaids were shuffling around, making sure that everything was to perfection, including me.

"Giorgio, darling. Come here and fix Jillian's eye shadow," my mother ordered as she snapped her fingers.

"Of course, of course," he spoke as he came running over to me.

"My eyeshadow is fine, Giorgio. Please step away from me before I lose my shit." I casually smiled.

His eyes widened as he set down his shadow palette and slowly walked away. I took in a deep breath as I stared at myself in the full-length mirror, dressed in white from head to toe, in a wedding dress that I hated. A dress my mother picked out. This day had been planned since I was born and I should be happy, right? After all, it was my wedding day. The day every girl dreamed of.

The girl staring back at me was someone I didn't recognize. I didn't know her. Everyone who had ever known me knew her. But to me, she was a stranger. As everyone was hustling and bustling around, I slipped out the side door of the room and made my way down the hall, where I looked out into the church and saw Grant standing at the altar with his best man, Paris. I was numb. Completely numb with no feeling inside me. When I looked down at my engagement ring, it had no meaning. As I removed it from my finger, I looked around and saw the side exit door of the church. This was my chance. It was now or never. I slipped back inside the dressing room.

"There you are, darling. It's time to line up. The ceremony is about to begin."

"I'll be out in a minute, Mom. I just want to be alone for a few minutes to calm my nerves."

"Now, Jillian dear, there's nothing to be nervous about. You've waited your whole life for this day."

I flashed her my fake smile. A smile that I had perfected over the years.

"I know. I just need a few moments. Okay?"

"Okay. We'll be outside the door, waiting for you."

As soon as everyone left, I grabbed my purse, took my phone out, and dialed a cab to pick me up at Pier 59. After doing a factory reset on my phone, I threw it down on the chair and laid my ring next to it. Turning around, I took one last look at the stranger in the mirror. Ripping the veil off my head, I quietly slipped out the other door and left the church without anyone noticing me. Nerves flooded throughout my body as I ran to the limo, climbed inside, and told the driver to step on it.

Pulling up to Pier 59, I climbed out of the limo and straight into the cab.

"Where to, lady?" the driver asked as he gave me a strange look.

"The Travelodge on 6th Avenue. And I'll need you to wait for me because I'm going to the airport."

"Sure. Okay."

As soon as he pulled up to the hotel, I told him that I'd be a few minutes and took the elevator to the second floor. Inserting the key card into the lock, I stepped inside the room and stripped out of my wedding dress. Unzipping the suitcase that was lying on the bed, I changed into a black maxi dress, slipped my feet into my black flip-flops, unpinned my brown hair, threw it up in a ponytail, and grabbed my other purse, which had my wallet and new phone in it. I took my luggage down to the lobby, handed it to the cab driver and climbed inside.

The reality of what I'd done finally set in and tears began to stream down my face. The emptiness I'd felt inside me for so long was still there, even though I was free. Free from the rope that my parents had tied around my neck since the day I was born. My mind was cluttered with chaos and racing a mile a minute, and the perfect wedding that was twenty-four years in the making was ruined. It wasn't my fault. How could I marry someone I didn't love? I could no longer pretend to be the happy, perfect Jillian Bell that everyone believed I was. A weight had been lifted off my shoulders and a new life was about to emerge. A life that I would be solely responsible for creating.

As I walked through the airport, pulling my carry-on behind me, I realized that I hadn't eaten a single thing all day. My mother had told me that if I ate before the ceremony, I would bloat and that was the only thing the guests would be focusing on. I was starving, so I stopped at La Pisa Café and ordered a panini and a bag of chips. As I was sat down and took a single bite of my panini, I pushed the button on my phone to check the time. *Shit.* My flight was already boarding. Setting my panini down on the plate, I shoved the bag of chips into my purse, grabbed my carry-on, and headed to my gate. When I reached the gate, I noticed it said the flight was going to Houston, Texas. Looking at my boarding pass, I asked the attendant behind the desk where the flight to LAX was.

"That flight was moved to Gate C24."

"Since when?" I asked abruptly.

"About thirty minutes ago." She politely smiled.

"But that's all the way at the other end of the airport and it's boarding now!"

"Then I suggest you run. An announcement was made overhead."

Shaking my head, I started to run through the airport to gate C24. This was my punishment, my karma for leaving Grant at the altar. Instead of sitting down with him and my parents, I took the coward's way out and ran and I was still running. This was unbelievable. Who does that sort of thing? A person who's been held a prisoner all her life for far too long and snaps. That's who. Just as I made it to the gate, they were getting ready to close the doors.

"WAIT!" I shouted breathlessly as I handed the attendant my boarding pass.

"You're lucky. You made it just in time."

Stepping onto the packed plane, I stopped dead in my tracks when I saw the person who was in the scat next to mine.

"Ah, shit," I silently spoke to myself. This was definitely my punishment. Dark hair, business suit, face of a god punishment.

Taking in a deep breath, I opened the overhead and he looked up at me, his dark brown eyes locked on mine through my sunglasses.

"I don't think there's any room up there."

"I can see that," I spoke as I shut the overhead.

Suddenly, a flight attendant approached me and took my carry-on from my hand.

"I'll find a space for it. Just sit down. We're taking off now."

"Thank you. Can I get a glass of wine, please?"

"As soon as we're up in the air, I'll bring you one." She gently smiled.

The man sitting next to me stood up so I could get to my seat with ease. Removing the pillow and the blanket, I sat down and took in a deep breath.

"Are you a nervous flier?" he asked.

Slowly turning my head, I looked at him through the sunglasses that I was still wearing.

"No."

"Well, just the way you wanted a glass of wine before you even sat down led me to believe you were."

Seriously? What business was it of his if I wanted a glass of wine?

"It's just been a really shitty day," I spoke as I looked out the window.

"I'm sorry to hear that. I hope it gets better for you." He politely smiled and then went back to looking at his phone.

As the plane lifted off the ground, I stared at the life I was leaving behind. A life that was never truly mine to begin with. My heart started racing and my skin became heated. Reaching up, I twisted the knob to the air vent as the rush of cool air poured down on me and I let out a breath.

"I thought you weren't a nervous flier," the man spoke.

"It's not the flight." I laid my head against the window.

Chapter Two
Jillian

"Here you go, miss," the flight attendant spoke as she handed me my wine.

"Thank you."

I didn't waste any time gulping down half the glass. I needed it more than I thought I did. Realizing that I still had my sunglasses on, I removed them and set them in my purse.

"You've been crying," the man who was all too fucking nosey, but seriously hot as fuck, especially with that light stubble across his jaw, spoke.

"How do you know that?" I asked with an attitude.

"Your makeup." He swept his finger under his eye.

Sighing, I took out the compact from my purse and opened it. *Ugh.* He was right. I looked like a raccoon. So much for the waterproof mascara Giorgio put on me. I got up from my seat and went to the bathroom. After cleaning myself up and reapplying my eyeliner and mascara, I sat down in my seat and looked at him.

"Better?" I spoke sarcastically.

He gave me a small but incredible smile. "I didn't think it looked bad before."

Looking down, my heart skipped a beat. This was the last thing I needed; to sit next to a sexy man who was trying to flirt with me just hours after I left my entire life behind and my fiancé standing at the altar.

"So, where are you traveling to?" he asked as I stared out the window.

"Hawaii," I replied.

"Me too. Are you traveling alone?"

"Yeah." I sighed. "Listen, I don't mean to be rude or anything, but I'm really not in a talkative mood."

"I understand. Sorry. After all, you did have a shitty day and I know when I have a shitty day, I'm not in the mood to talk either."

"Good. I'm happy you understand." I sighed.

I signaled for the flight attendant and asked her for another glass of wine. Bringing my knees up, I placed the pillow against the window and leaned my head against it. I was exhausted, both physically and mentally. My mind couldn't help but wonder what was happening back in Seattle. The look on my mother's face when she found I was gone. The embarrassment on Grant's face when I never walked down the aisle. The whispers of the guests who gave up their time to attend a wedding that never happened. A tear ran down my cheek, and not because I was sad about what I'd done. I wasn't entirely sure why the tear fell from my eye. Maybe it was because I wasn't a robot anymore, looking at my life from the outside. I no longer had to pretend to be happy, and every smile that crossed my lips from now on would be real and genuine.

"Here." The man handed me a tissue.

Taking it from him, I wiped my eyes.

"Thanks."

"You're welcome. I wouldn't want your mascara to run again." He smirked.

A smile fell upon my face. A real smile. A smile that made me feel good inside.

"Here's your wine." The flight attendant handed me my glass. "May I get you anything else?"

"Is there a meal service on this flight?"

"No. I'm sorry. Light snacks only, but there will be a meal served on your connecting flight from LAX."

The man reached down in the small bag he had under the seat in front of him and pulled out a protein bar.

"Eat this." He handed it to me.

"Thanks, but no, I'm fine."

"Obviously, you're hungry. Don't you like protein bars?" He smiled.

"I like protein bars. I eat them almost every day. Thank you for the offer, but I can wait."

He shrugged. "Suit yourself. If you're not going to eat it, then I will." He removed the wrapper and took a bite.

"You don't even know me and you're offering me your protein bar. Why?" I asked out of curiosity.

"Because you had a shitty day. It's the least I could do to try and make your day a little better. That way, you can tell everyone that a nice gentleman on the plane gave you his protein bar because you were hungry."

I let out a light laugh and shook my head. God, it felt good to laugh.

"See." He smiled. "I think I just made your day a little less shitty."

I laughed again. "Maybe I'll just have a piece."

He broke the bar in half and handed it to me.

"Thank you—" I cocked my head and narrowed my eye.

"Drew. Drew Westbrook." He stuck out his hand.

"Nice to meet you, Drew. Jillian Bell." I politely placed my hand in his.

"Jillian. That's a beautiful name."

I could feel the heat rise in my cheeks as I thanked him. A heat that I'd never felt before.

"I think I'm going to watch a movie," I spoke as I took the headphones out of the package the flight attendant gave me.

Looking at his watch, Drew spoke. "You won't have enough time. We're landing in about an hour."

"Oh. Okay, then I think I'll just take a nap. Could you please wake me when we land?"

"Of course." He nodded.

****

Drew

Jillian Bell. A beautiful name for an incredibly beautiful woman. The minute she stepped onto the plane, I took notice of her. Her brown hair with the subtle blonde highlights pulled back in a ponytail and her five-foot-six small-framed but very toned body that sported the black maxi dress she wore to perfection. I hated that she kept on those damn Gucci sunglasses for so long because I needed to see her eyes. When she finally took them off and I saw the ocean blue staring back at me, I was left breathless, even with the mascara stains underneath them. She was broken, that much I could tell, and there was a part of me that wanted to reach out and fix her. A complete stranger. Something I didn't do. I was curious as to why she was traveling to Hawaii alone. Something happened. A break-up, perhaps? I wanted to know and I was going to find out more about Jillian Bell before our plane landed in Hawaii.

As she rested her head on the pillow, I couldn't help but stare at her. Even while she attempted to sleep, she didn't seem at peace. I sighed as I looked down at my iPad and sorted through some emails. Every time she stirred, I looked over at her to make sure she was okay.

Chapter Three
Jillian

I awoke to the soft touch of a hand on my shoulder and the soft whisper of my name.

"Jillian, we've landed."

"Already?" I yawned.

Drew chuckled. "Yes, already."

Once the plane entered the gate, the flight attendant handed me my carry-on bag and Drew stepped aside to let me out.

"Ladies first." He gave a charming smile.

"Thank you."

As I stepped off the plane, I looked around for a monitor to see which gate my next flight was at.

"Jillian?" Drew spoke as he approached me.

"Yeah?"

"We have an hour and a half layover until our next flight. How about we grab something to eat? I know that half a protein bar didn't do much for you and the idea of dinner on the plane is a little revolting. Totally not my idea of fine dining."

Drew Westbrook seemed like a really nice guy. A really hot and sexy nice guy. His six-foot stature, dark hair, smoldering brown eyes to match, the stubble he sported on his face, and overall demeanor was refreshing. A little panty soaking but refreshing. Was he hitting on me? Probably, but it didn't matter. Guys were off limits to me and would be for a very long time. Not until I found me, would I even consider finding a guy.

"Sure. Why not." I smiled.

"Great. Is there anything in particular you're in the mood for?"

"A nice thick juicy burger and a plate full of French fries."

He narrowed his right eye. "Really? I wouldn't have thought you ate stuff like that, considering how fit you look."

"I normally don't, but today calls for comfort food."

"I see. Okay. A nice thick juicy burger and a plate full of French fries it is."

As we headed in the direction of our gate, we stopped and took a seat at Umami Burger.

"What can I get you?" the waitress asked.

"I'll have the LAX burger, please."

"Everything on it?" she asked.

"Yes. And whatever you have on tap." I smiled.

"And for you, sir?"

"I'll have the veggie burger and whatever you have on tap."

"The veggie burger?" I smirked.

"Is something wrong with a veggie burger?" He cocked his head.

"No. Nothing at all." I snickered.

"I didn't take you for a beer kind of girl."

"Oh really? And what kind of girl did you take me for?"

"The kind of girl who drinks fine wines, fruity cocktails, and expensive champagne."

I looked down as I ran my finger and thumb along where my ring once sat.

"I like a beer every now and again."

He was right about me. I did drink fine wines, fruity cocktails, and expensive champagne. Ever since I could remember, my mother used to tell me that beer was for the lower class; that it was a cheap man's drink and I had an image to uphold. I could never drink a beer around my parents or Grant. He was just as bad as they were, only drinking his scotch or bourbon on the rocks and holding his glass in such a prissy manner as to alert everyone he was the upper class and not to be fucked with.

"Earth to Jillian." Drew waved his hand in front of my face.

I looked up at him and lightly shook my head. "Sorry. What were you saying?"

"You seemed lost in thought. Care to talk about it?"

The waitress set down our beers in front of us and I quickly took a large sip.

"No." I smiled as I set down my glass.

His eyes narrowed at me as he studied me for a moment.

"Who are you, Jillian Bell?"

Tilting my head to the side and giving a light shrug, I spoke, "I have no clue."

A confused look swept over his face, and before he had a chance to say anything, the waitress set our burgers in front of us.

"How's that veggie burger?" I asked.

"It's good. How's that grease-dripping burger you're eating?"

"Fantastic," I spoke with a mouthful of food.

Drew let out a light chuckle. Once we finished eating, I leaned back in my chair and puffed out my cheeks.

"Oh my God. I'm so full."

Did I care that I had just scarfed down a burger, a plate of fries, and a beer in front of a sexy man that I had just met a couple of hours ago? No. I didn't even give it a second thought. I was over what anybody thought of me.

"We better get to our gate," Drew spoke as he pulled out his wallet and threw some cash on the table.

Reaching into my purse, I pulled out some money.

"I got it, Jillian." He smiled.

"No. No. I'm paying for my own." I set the dollar bills on the table.

Drew picked them up and placed them back in my hand.

"I said I got it. See? Now I've once again made your shitty day a little less shitty." He grinned.

I couldn't help but smile as I stared into his deep dark brown eyes. He was a really nice guy. Or was he just trying to get into my pants? Either way, I let him pay. He could be nice all he wanted but he wouldn't get a piece of me, even though the thought of his muscular strong body on top of mine was enticing. *Shit.* I needed to stop thinking that.

As we boarded the plane for Hawaii, I took my seat next to an older woman who was dripping in gold and diamonds. She wore a Donna Karan suit, and when I looked down at her feet, I couldn't help but notice her Jimmy Choo's. Her hair was secured in a perfect bun and her makeup was immaculate. She reminded me too much of my mother. Drew's seat was two rows behind me and I admit that I was a little disappointed he wasn't sitting next to me.

"Excuse me, ma'am?" Drew spoke as he stood in the aisle. "Would you mind switching seats with me? I have a lovely window seat two rows back."

"I'm fine where I'm at," she spoke with an attitude, not looking up from her magazine.

I looked up at Drew, gave him a wink, and motioned for him to go sit back in his seat. Suddenly, I began to cough loudly until the woman looked over.

"Are you all right?" she asked.

"No." I coughed in her face.

She leaned to the side of her seat, away from me as I kept coughing.

"Can you please cover your mouth?"

"Oh sorry. It happens so much that sometimes I forget."

As I coughed in my hand, I placed it on her arm.

"I'm sorry, but once I start, it could go on for hours. So I want to apologize in advance for the disruption it may cause you during our six-hour flight."

She looked down at my hand, which was touching the fabric of her suit, and then back up at me. Grabbing her purse, she got up from her seat and, before I knew it, Drew was sitting next to me.

"Well played, Jillian." He winked.

"Thank you." I smiled. "I didn't want to sit next to her anyway. She reminds me of my mother."

"Is that a bad thing?" His brow arched.

"Yeah. It is." I looked away.

Chapter Four
Jillian

Once the plane took off, the flight attendant took our dinner order, which consisted of either a chicken enchilada or a salmon salad. Drew opted for the salmon salad and I declined both. Not only was I still full from that ginormous burger, I didn't like enchiladas and there was no way I was eating salmon from an airplane.

"I thought plane food revolted you?" I smirked.

"It does, but that veggie burger didn't seem to fill me up and the salmon salad doesn't sound too bad."

"You should have had the big thick greasy burger like me."

"Yeah. Maybe I should have." He winked.

"What do you do for work?" I asked with curiosity.

"I own and run a technology company."

I knew he was in corporate just by the suit he was wearing. He had "corporate man" written all over him. One thing that caught me by surprise was the fact that he owned the company.

"Nice. How old are you?" I cocked my head.

He laughed. "I don't think it's polite to ask someone their age."

"Wrong. It's not polite to ask a woman her age, but for a man, it's no holds barred."

"So why is it wrong to ask a woman?" His brow raised.

"Because women are more sensitive to the age question than men. It's in our genes."

"Ah. I see. Well, to answer your question, I'm thirty. And now, you'll answer my question, impolite or not. How old are you?"

"I'm twenty-four."

"Really?" He frowned. "You don't look a day over eighteen." His lips gave way to a small smile.

Rolling my eyes, I couldn't help but laugh. "Is that why you're being so nice to me, because you thought I was a naïve eighteen-year-old who just blossomed into a legal adult with no baggage that you could manipulate in the palm of your hand?" I smirked.

"First of all, eighteen year olds aren't my thing. They are way too immature, legal adult or not, and second of all, I'm just a nice guy all the way around." He winked.

"That you are, Mr. Westbrook." My lips gave way to a small smile.

The flight attendant set Drew's salmon salad down in front of him. I took one look at it and sighed.

"You're really going to eat that?"

"Of course." He stabbed his fork into the salad and took a bite. "It's delicious."

"It is not! I can tell by the look on your face and the way you're trying to choke it down."

He shrugged. "Okay. It's not very appetizing."

"Oh. Is that cheesecake?" I asked as I pointed to the small plate on his tray.

"It looks like it. Do you want it?"

"Don't you?" I asked.

"I'm not a big cheesecake kind of person. So, please, be my guest. I'll have to ask the attendant for another fork."

"No need." I smiled as I reached over, picked it up with my hands, and took a bite.

Drew's face twisted as he watched me.

"What? It's not a big piece. It's bite size." I finished it off with one more bite. "Thank you for once again making my shitty day a little less shitty." I grinned.

"You're welcome." He nodded. "I'm surprised you're still hungry after that large burger, a beer, your fries, and mine."

Without even thinking, I spoke, "Well, after starving myself for the last six months to make sure I didn't gain an ounce so I could fit into my wedding—" I paused and then turned my head towards the window.

Drew didn't say a word, which was a good thing because I wasn't about to get into something so personal about myself with a stranger.

"So, what do you do for a living?" he asked to change the subject.

"I'm a lawyer. Well, not technically yet. I still have to take the bar." Which I had no plans to ever do.

"Impressive. Where did you attend law school?"

"Yale."

"Wow. Now I'm really impressed." He smiled. "Did you just graduate?"

"Yep. Two weeks ago and at the top of my class."

"Your parents must be very proud of you. That's quite an accomplishment."

"They are." *Not now they aren't*, I thought to myself.

The flight attendant walked over and took Drew's tray from him as I pulled out the headphones from my purse.

"I think I'll watch a movie now," I spoke.

"All right. I have some work to do." He pulled out his iPad.

****

Drew

A lawyer. Wow, not only was she beautiful but extremely smart. I caught the part about her wedding dress, which piqued my curiosity, but I could tell after she slipped that she was upset, so I didn't ask her any more about it. I got the impression that her fiancé broke it off with her and that was why she was so broken. As for Hawaii, she was probably trying to escape the pain. I found her refreshing and funny. She had a wit about her that captivated me. Who would ever break up with someone like her? If she were mine, I would have held on to her forever.

As I was doing some work on my iPad, the plane hit some bad turbulence. Jillian reached over and grabbed my arm.

"Are you okay?" I asked.

"Sorry. Turbulence just freaks me the fuck out." She inhaled deeply and laid her head back.

"Don't apologize. My arm is here for you whenever you need it." I smiled.

The plane leveled out and it seemed we were in the clear. Letting go of my arm, Jillian continued to watch her movie and I went back to work.

****

Jillian

Just as I started to relax again, the plane abruptly dropped and the pilot announced that we were heading into some severe storms and turbulence was going to a problem for a short while. The seatbelt light went on and all the flight attendants were commanded to sit in their seats until we got through it. I wasn't sure if *I* could get through it. As I felt the plane going up and down, I grabbed on to Drew's arm again. For now, he was my safety and there was no way I was letting go. Anxiety had started to kick in and I found it difficult to breathe.

"Hey. Relax. It's going to okay," Drew said as he placed his hand on mine. "Let's talk. Tell me something. Anything."

He was trying to distract me and I appreciated him for it. He could see I was struggling to calm the fuck down.

"Breathe, Jillian." His eyes burnt into mine.

My heart was pounding out of my chest and I was sweating.

"Talk to me," he spoke with seriousness.

"I left my fiancé at the altar today. I didn't even tell him that I couldn't marry him. I just up and left without anyone noticing a couple of minutes before I was to walk down the aisle. I couldn't marry him. I don't love him. I never did. It was too much. Between my parents and him, I just couldn't take it anymore," I blurted out. "And now, this is my punishment. We're going to crash and I'm going to die and go to Hell for it."

Drew stared at me with a shocked expression on his face. He didn't know what to say because I was sure his whole perception of me had just changed in that moment.

"We aren't going to crash, you're not going to die, and you certainly aren't going to Hell because you left your fiancé."

After he spoke those words, the plane leveled out and once again became steady. The pilot came on the overhead and said we were in the clear and thanked us for our cooperation. Letting out a sigh of relief, I began to calm down and regain my breath.

"See. It was just a little turbulence. It's over now." He smiled.

"I'm sorry for just blurting that out."

"It's okay. You thought you were going to die, so you had to tell someone. Do you want to talk about it?" he asked in a soothing voice.

"That's basically it. Today was my wedding day and I ran."

"If you never loved him, why did you accept his proposal?"

"Because I had no choice. He was my fiancé since I was a child. Planned by my parents and his. He was the one I had to marry."

"Wait a minute." He shook his head. "Was this an arranged marriage?"

I laughed. "If you really stop to think about it, I guess it was. His parents and my parents have been best friends since they were teenagers. He is the heir to his father's law firm and I am the daughter of the prestigious Donald Bell of DB Simpson & Co."

"You mean one of the largest global financial firms, DB Simpson & Co?"

"Yep. That's the one."

"Wow. Oh boy. Wow."

"See. You're speechless."

"Not really. I mean, why would you marry someone you're not in love with? I just don't understand why you didn't say something before the wedding."

"Because I never had any control over my own life. From the day I was born, my life had already been planned out. Where I would go to school, who my friends would be, who I could and could not socialize with, and my career. Shit. I don't even want to be a lawyer."

"I take it you're an only child?"

"Yeah. Well, sort of. That's another story." I shook my head.

Drew looked at his watch. "We have a couple of hours left."

"Thanks, but I don't really want to talk about it. It's just that I never was allowed to make my own decisions. My mom and Grant's mom planned the entire wedding. I didn't have a say in anything, not even my wedding dress. The one I wanted wasn't expensive enough and my mother said it made me look fat. So she picked the dress she liked and I just agreed to it. I didn't care and I didn't have any fight in me. Going against my parents was a losing battle."

"And now?" he asked.

"I guess you could say I snapped." I gave a small smile. "I don't know who I am, Drew. Every time I look in a mirror, I see a total stranger staring back at me."

"So you're going to Hawaii. Why?" He cocked his head.

"I needed to escape and what better place than Hawaii. I'm starting my life over and, little by little, I'm going to find out who Jillian Bell really is."

The corners of his mouth curved upwards. "Good for you."

"Thanks. It's really liberating."

"So what about your parents and Grant?"

"Who knows and who cares? I don't think he even loved me anyway. He was a cheater and a liar. Hell, his bachelor party was last weekend in Vegas and he slept with two strippers at the same time." I looked down.

"Ouch. What a dick. I'm sorry."

"Don't be. I'm not. I'm feeling really tired from that whole turbulence experience. I'm going to try and get some sleep. So,

would you wake me if I'm still sleeping when the plane lands?"
I bit down on my bottom lip.

"Of course I will, and if you need my shoulder to lie on, it's available."

"Thanks, but the window is fine."

I propped the pillow against the window and laid my head down against it.

Chapter Five
Drew

Wow, her story really hit a spot in my heart and I felt sorry for her. I could feel her pain as she talked about leaving her fiancé at the altar, and her parents, shit, I couldn't imagine growing up like that. Just as we were about to land, Jillian opened her eyes and looked around.

"We'll be landing in a couple of minutes. I can't believe I'm landing in Hawaii in the dark." I smirked.

"You had to have known when you booked the flight," she spoke.

"This wasn't my original flight. My other flight was delayed due to mechanical issues and then it got cancelled. This is the flight they put me on. I was supposed to arrive around three thirty pm, not nine fifty pm."

"This was the only flight that had first class available when I booked it."

"And when did you book this flight?" I asked.

"Two weeks ago. It was a backup, just in case. And as you can see, the just in case happened."

When the plane arrived at the gate, I took Jillian's carry-on bag from the overhead and handed it to her. After grabbing mine, I took a step back and let her out first.

"I'm going to use the bathroom before I head to baggage claim."

"Oh. Okay. I can wait for you," she spoke.

"You go ahead."

I didn't know how to say it. This shouldn't have been so hard and I didn't understand why it was. Maybe because we shared a connection on the plane. Who the hell knew.

"Actually, my girlfriend is meeting me. She flew in this morning."

****

Jillian

Awkward moment. Was I surprised? No. I didn't expect a man like him to be single and I never asked him why he was flying to Hawaii alone. I didn't know what to say.

"That's great." My lips gave way to the smile that I had perfected. "Well, I guess this is goodbye. Thank you, Drew, for making my shitty day a little less shitty. It was nice to meet you."

His lips formed a small smile as he held out his hand to me.

"It was nice to meet you too, Jillian. I hope everything works out for you and you find yourself."

"Thank you." I lightly shook his hand.

As I walked away, Drew called my name.

"Jillian?"

I turned around and took one last look at him.

"Do me a favor. Please be careful while you're here. No matter where you go, there are always some crazy people around."

"Don't worry about me. I'll be fine." I gave him a small wave and headed to baggage claim.

There was a part of me that was sad about saying goodbye to Drew Westbrook. He was the first nice person I'd met on my self-discovery journey. Talking to him for most of the day made me feel good. For the first time in my life, I felt happy inside. When I arrived at the baggage claim area, I saw a nice-looking gentleman holding up a sign with my name on it.

"That's me." I smiled.

"Ah, welcome to Hawaii, Miss Bell. I'm Kaleo, and it's my pleasure to drive you to your hotel."

"Nice to meet you, Kaleo."

"Your luggage will be coming out right over here."

As we were waiting for the luggage to be unloaded, I happened to glance over and saw Drew hugging a tall, blonde-haired woman. A lump formed in the back of my throat and I quickly looked away. I just wanted to get the hell out of here and to the hotel so I could climb into bed and sleep my troubles away. Finally, I saw my luggage come around and Kaleo picked it up and led me to the sedan that was parked right outside the doors. I had no choice but to pass by Drew and his girlfriend, so I kept my eyes looking straight ahead and pretended not to see them.

When Kaleo pulled up to the Kahala Hotel & Resort, he removed my bags from the trunk and the bellhop in front of the hotel grabbed them.

"Welcome to the Kahala Hotel & Resort." He smiled.

I checked myself in, and when I turned around, I saw Drew and his girlfriend heading to the same elevators I was. *Shit. Fuck. Shit.* Why did he have to be staying at the same hotel?

"Hello." He nodded.

"Hey." I smiled. "Nice to see you again."

The tall blonde narrowed her eye at me and I could see her claws emerge.

"Jess, this is Jillian. Her seat was next to mine on the plane."

"Oh. Hello." She extended her well-manicured hand with an unsure smile and daggering eyes.

"Nice to meet you, Jess."

We stepped inside the elevator and the bellhop pushed the button for the Presidential Suite. No one spoke a word. This was awkward and there was no reason that it should have been. But then, why did I feel like I had done something wrong? As soon as the elevator doors opened, I stepped out and spoke to them, "Enjoy your vacation."

"You too," Drew replied while Jess gave me a slight nod.

Opening the door to my suite, the bellhop set my bags down in the bedroom. I reached in my pocket and pulled out some cash.

"Thank you for bringing my bags up."

"Thank you, Miss Bell. Enjoy your stay with us. If you need anything at all, please let us know."

I grabbed my phone from my purse and looked at the time. It was almost eleven. I promised my best friend, Kellan, that I would call him as soon as I got settled. It was two a.m. in Seattle, and I took my chances that he was still up.

"Hello," he answered.

"Hey. It's so good to hear a familiar voice."

"I've been waiting for your call. How are you? I've been worried sick."

"I'm okay. So what happened?"

"Oh, Jillian. I don't even know where to start. Your mom and dad are pissed as hell, and Grant, I just think that little douchebag was more embarrassed than anything. Your mom came to me and asked me if I knew about the little stunt you pulled."

"Were those her exact words?"

"Yes. I'd never seen her so angry. Her face was so red that I was sure she was going to drop dead of a heart attack right there in the church. Grant made an announcement and told all the guests that this was just a misunderstanding and he'd get it sorted out. I'll be honest with you, Jill, I don't think you'll ever be able to come back here."

"I don't ever plan on it. You know that and I know that. Listen, I'm exhausted and I just want to go to sleep. I'll call you tomorrow."

"Okay, baby girl. Sweet dreams and I'm proud of you. I love you."

"I love you too, Kellan, and thank you for everything you've done for me."

After ending the call, I unzipped my suitcase and pulled out my nightgown. Once I changed, I pulled back the covers, climbed into the luxurious king-sized bed, and pulled the sheets up over me, holding the edges with a tight grip. A million different emotions were going through my head and I just needed to turn my brain off. Easier said than done as I tossed and turned all night.

****

Drew

She's very pretty," Jess spoke as the elevator doors shut.

"I didn't notice," I lied.

"Oh, come on, Drew. Who the hell wouldn't notice a girl like her?"

Jess was raring to start a fight. I could tell and I was in no mood. I was tired and I didn't plan to be up all night arguing with her.

"Jess, I'm warning you. We aren't going to go through this again. For fuck sakes," I spoke as I opened the door to the Imperial Suite, "I couldn't help that her seat was next to mine."

"Did you talk to her?" she asked as she headed towards the bathroom.

"Of course I did. We were on a six-hour flight." I didn't dare tell her that we also sat next to each other on the plane from Seattle.

"Did she come here alone?" she asked as she stood in front of the mirror and took off her makeup.

"Yes. She was supposed to get married today but couldn't go through with it."

"Wow. It seems like you got her life story."

Slowly closing my eyes, I took in a deep breath.

"Not really."

"Why would she tell you that? A total stranger? Who does that shit?"

"Apparently, a woman who needed to talk to someone."

"Did she hit on you?" she asked as she turned the light off and climbed into bed.

"No. She didn't hit on me and you're being ridiculous right now. Listen, you need to stop being so jealous of every woman who looks my way. Have I ever given you a reason to mistrust me?"

"No."

"Exactly." I reached down and kissed her lips. "Now get some sleep. I'm exhausted and had a really long day. I didn't plan to get in this late."

"But I've been looking forward to having sex with you all day." Her hand reached down and rubbed my cock.

"Not tonight, Jess. I'm way too tired."

"What a great start to this vacation." She huffed.

"Can you please for once in your life think about somebody besides yourself?"

She turned the other way and I didn't care. I sighed as I placed my hands behind my head and stared up at the ceiling. The only woman on my mind at the moment was Jillian.

Chapter Six
Jillian

The sun peered through the window as I opened the curtains and greeted the warm beautiful day. Staring at the full ocean view from my window, I smiled at the peace and serenity I felt at that moment. Sitting down on the bed, I opened up my laptop; there was someone I needed to check in on and talk to.

"Hey, you. I've been waiting for you to skype." Kristen smiled.

"I'm sorry. By time I got to the hotel last night, it was late, and you're six hours ahead, so I didn't want to wake you."

"I can't believe you did it."

"Me either. How are you feeling?"

"Same. I have chemo tomorrow and then another scan next week. But don't worry about me. I'll be fine. You need to focus on you and you only."

"You know I'm always worried about you." I pouted.

"Well, don't be. I want you to have fun in Hawaii and focus on you. I'll be here when you come to New York."

"Is Noah taking good care of you?"

"He always does." She smiled.

"Okay. I'm going to go so you can get some rest. I wish you could be here with me."

"Me too. But no worries. We'll take a trip one of these days."

After saying goodbye, I rubbed my hand down my face. The guilt I felt about not flying straight to New York was eating at me. Kristen wouldn't hear of it and told me to go somewhere for a while to collect my thoughts before settling in to my new life. She was one of the strongest women I knew and I couldn't wait to see her.

After I took a shower, I curled the ends of my long brown hair, slipped into my floral spaghetti-strapped sundress, and headed downstairs to the restaurant for breakfast. When I walked in, I saw Drew and Jess sitting at a table. He was reading the newspaper and she was looking at her phone. Sighing, I asked the hostess to seat me on the other side of the restaurant.

As I sipped on my coffee, my phone rang, and it was Kellan.

"Hi there," I answered.

"Hey. Sorry to bother you on your vacay, but I have to ask. You haven't used any of your old credit cards, right?"

"No. I haven't. I've been paying cash or using my new card."

"Good. Your mom paid me a little visit earlier and demanded to know where you were. I really had to talk my way out of that one. I even had to cry. She and your father are checking all your credit cards, rental car places, airports, hotels, and your bank account."

"They can check all they want. They won't find anything."

"Apparently, the limo driver spilled the beans and told them he dropped you off at Pier 59."

"That asshole. I paid him good money to keep his mouth shut."

"Well, your parents paid more to get the truth. But he didn't tell them you got into a cab. He just said that when he dropped you off, he saw you walking down the street on foot."

"Did you get rid of the dress?" I asked.

"Yeah. I went to the hotel last night, boxed it up, and sent it off to that girl in Wisconsin this morning."

"Thank you."

As I looked up, I saw Drew looking over at me. I gave a small smile and nod.

"Hello? Jill? Are you there?"

"Sorry."

"Are you okay? Are you having second thoughts about everything?"

"God no! But I'm fine. It's just I met this guy on the plane yesterday and then, when we landed in Los Angeles, we grabbed a bite to eat. We sat together again on the plane to Hawaii. Now he's staying at the same hotel and I just saw him looking at me from across the restaurant."

"Oh. Meow. Is he hot?"

I smiled. "Yeah. He is incredibly hot and he's here with his girlfriend."

"Damn."

"No damn, Kellan. A guy is the last thing I need. Remember, I'm starting my life over. It's a guy-free zone, at least for the next ten years or so."

"I think ten years is a little ridiculous, Jilly Bean."

"Nah. Ten should give me enough time to figure out who I am. There will be no exceptions."

"If you say so. Go enjoy Hawaii. I just wanted to update you on the evil queen."

"Thanks for letting me know. I'll talk to you later."

As I was eating my breakfast, I saw Drew and Jess get up from their table and head out of the restaurant with his hand on the small of her back. I won't lie and say that my mind didn't wonder what it would be like to have him as a boyfriend. The thought of dating scared me. I had only been with one guy my entire life: Grant. *Ugh.* The thought of him made my stomach feel sick. He came from an influential family of lawyers. And yes, we did attend Yale together. I think it was his and my parents' way of keeping an eye on me. His father, a hotshot lawyer, owned his own high power firm, and as soon as Grant passed the bar, he would immediately become a partner and then take over completely when his father retired. I had no clue how he was going to be a lawyer since he never bothered to listen to what anyone said unless it benefited him. He was the true definition of a narcissist. He wasn't even all that good looking. I mean, he was cute in his own five-foot-eight way. He was your typical preppy boy. Short dark hair that swept to the side, blue eyes, and certainly no muscles anywhere to be found on his body. He always wore polo shirts, which I hated, and occasionally, he would tie a sweater around his neck. If you looked up the definition of a snob in the dictionary, you'd see his picture full front and center. He looked down on people who didn't have the kind of wealth he had and he was never ashamed to flaunt it. He was a cheater, a liar, and didn't care about anyone but himself. Now let's talk about sex. The thought made me shudder. His penis. Well, let's just say that half the time, I couldn't even feel it. I faked more orgasms than I had actual ones, and the actual ones were compliments of myself. He thought he was the man in the bedroom, but the truth was, he was just a boy who didn't know what the fuck he was doing. We hadn't had sex in months. It became draining trying to make up excuses why I didn't want to. I was too tired, I had a headache, I had an infection, I was ovulating, I was on my period, I forgot to take my birth control pill the night before. You name it, I used it. Having sex with him was something I dreaded. It wasn't a partnership. It was more about him satisfying his own needs.

I had meant what I said to Kellan on the phone. My new life and journey that I was about to embark on was about me. I didn't care if "Mr. Right" walked up to me at this very moment. Guys weren't going to be a part of my journey. Not for a very long time. This was a solo mission. My entire life had been in the hands of other people and now, I was taking it back. After finishing breakfast, I decided to do a little stand-up paddle boarding. After I headed up to my suite, I changed into my black bikini, threw my cover-up on me, grabbed a towel, and headed out the door. When the doors to the elevator opened, I saw Drew and Jess standing there.

"Hi." I smiled.

"Hi," Drew spoke with a small smile.

"Hello." Jess looked me up and down. "Are you going to the pool?" she asked.

"Paddle boarding," I replied.

"Ugh, I hate paddle boarding."

"Well, it's not for everyone." I slightly rolled my eyes.

When the elevator doors opened, I stepped out and spoke, "Have a great day."

"You too," Drew replied.

While they walked away, I couldn't help but stare at his attire. Black swim trunks that were just the right length, a tight light gray t-shirt that hugged his body in all the right places, and flip-flops. He looked smoking hot and I won't lie and say my bikini bottoms didn't get a little wet. *Ugh.* Shaking my head and entering back into reality, I walked over to where the paddle boards were.

"Can I paddle board out to that little island?" I pointed.

"You sure can. There's a couple spots where you can sit down and get some sun if you want."

"Great." I smiled.

A feeling of peace overtook me as I got on the paddle board and began to make my way towards the island. As I was sitting there with my knees hugging my chest, I stared out into the ocean and listened to the serene sound of the waves. I had been to Hawaii many times growing up, and every time I visited, I felt the same peace that resided in me now, but that sense of feeling flew away the minute we stepped on the plane to go home.

Staring out and taking in the warmth of the sun that enveloped me, I noticed a man who kept falling off his paddle board heading towards the island. As I strained my eyes to get a better look, it seemed that man looked like Drew. He saw me staring at him as he sat on his board and put his arms out as if he was giving up. Laughing, I grabbed my board and paddled out to him.

"What are you doing?" I asked.

"I was trying to get to the island to come and say hi, but it just wasn't working out."

"Have you never been on a paddle board before?"

"No. Actually, I haven't." He sighed.

"Where's Jess?"

"She came down with a migraine and went back to the room to lie down. I was sitting down at the pool and remembered you had said you were going paddle boarding, so I thought I'd give it a try."

"How did you know I was at that island?"

"I asked the guy at the rental place if he knew which direction you were headed and he said you had asked about the island. So, hi." He smiled.

"Hi." I grinned. "Do you think you can make it back to shore without falling in the water?"

"I don't think so. Maybe I should have had some lessons first."

"That probably would have been a good idea. You know you can just sit on your knees. You don't have to stand up if you're not comfortable."

"I thought about that, but then I'd look like an idiot out here. Look around; everyone is standing."

I couldn't help but laugh. "Okay, hand me your paddle and slowly stand up. Put your foot where your knee was. One foot at a time and make sure the nose doesn't dip up. Then, keep your feet hip width apart. The most important thing to remember is don't balance with your entire body, just your hips, and don't look down. Keep your head up and looking forward at all times."

Drew did exactly what I said and balanced himself.

"Good, now here's your paddle. Make sure you grip the top and stand tall. Don't slouch."

"Like this?" he asked.

"Yes. Perfect. Now follow me and use short strokes."

As we began to paddle board back to shore, I looked over and noticed he was going in the wrong direction. I busted out into laughter.

"You're going the wrong way!" I shouted.

"I can't help it. It's making me."

"You're paddling wrong. We're going to the left, so you want to paddle on the right."

"Oh. That makes sense." He smiled as he turned his board around.

Finally, we made it back to shore, and I was pleasantly surprised how Drew managed to stay on the whole time.

"That was quite an adventure." He grinned.

"Yeah. It sure was."

We returned our paddle boards and began walking towards the lobby of the hotel.

"I think I'm going to hang out at the pool," he spoke. "Care to join me?"

"I'm going to head back to the room and change. There's someone I have to go see."

"Okay. You have a friend here?"

"Yeah. He's an old friend that I visit every time I come here."

"You must visit a lot."

"Every couple of years since I was six years old. I actually consider Hawaii my second home."

"Nice. Have fun reconnecting with your friend."

"Thanks. Have fun at the pool or maybe go take a paddle boarding lesson." I winked.

He chuckled and I walked away and went back to my room.

Chapter Seven
Drew

She was so beautiful and she was all I thought about. I know, I was a bastard because I was in Hawaii with my girlfriend. But the truth was, we hadn't been getting along the past couple months and I'd wondered if she was even worth it anymore. After having a slight disagreement at the pool, Jess suddenly came down with a migraine. She was successfully ruining this trip and it had only been one day. We had been dating about a year and my feelings for her never grew into anything more. She was a very selfish and jealous person and I couldn't even smile politely at another woman without being accused of wanting to sleep with her. Her insecurities had been pushing me away for a while now and she knew it. This trip was her idea, and the reason we didn't fly together was because I had an emergency business meeting in Seattle that came up unexpectedly, and I needed to be there. So she took our original flight out of New York and I changed my flight to fly out of Seattle.

As I sipped on my Mai Tai at the pool, I couldn't get Jillian's smile out of my head. Her laughter was enough to brighten up anyone's life. She had touched me in a way that I had never felt before. From the moment she stepped on the plane, I felt a rush of something. I couldn't even tell you what the hell it was because it was something I'd never experienced before.

"Hey," Jess spoke as she sat down next to me.

"Hey. Are you feeling better?"

"A little. I'm sorry about earlier. I know it was all my fault and I just want this trip to be perfect. You've been so distant lately. We've been distant."

"I know." I sighed.

"I'm going to try harder, Drew. I promise. I love you, baby, and I want things to be good between us." She leaned over and brushed her lips against mine.

"Okay. Would you like a drink?"

She ran her finger down my chest. "Why don't we go back to the room and make love?"

"Are you feeling up to it?"

"Yes, and I know you're the perfect cure for me." She smiled.

****

Jess and I hadn't had sex in over a month and I wasn't really bothered by it. With the problems we'd been having and all the arguing, I wasn't in the mood. I would just put on some porn and take care of myself. I thought maybe having sex with her now would make me feel something or feel different, but it didn't and it didn't help that I had a problem staying hard. *Shit.* I never had that problem before and it bothered me.

"Don't be upset over it, Drew." She softly stroked my chest. "I know you've been under a lot of stress lately with the company and I've done my fair share in contributing to that stress."

I wanted to tell her that I didn't think stress had anything to do with it and that she was more than likely the reason why. Actually, Jillian was the reason why. I couldn't stop thinking about her and how it would feel to make love to her. The whole time I was fucking Jess, I was thinking about Jillian, and it needed to stop. I would never have a chance with her anyway. Not only had she just dumped her fiancé yesterday, she was starting over and embarking on a self-discovery journey to find herself.

"I'm not upset and you're right, I've been under a lot of stress lately," I lied.

"Well, we're just going to have to destress you, and the first thing I'm going to do to prove to you that I've changed is I'm going to invite that girl, what's her name?"

"What girl?"

"The one who left her fiancé at the altar?"

"Jillian?"

"Yes, I'm going to invite Jillian to have dinner with us before we leave."

Shit. That was not a good idea.

"You don't have to do that, Jess. This vacation is for the two of us."

"Don't be silly. I want to. She seems like a nice girl and she's here alone. I kind of feel sorry for her. I'm sure she's torn up by what she did and she could use some company."

****

Jillian

I rented a car and drove to Ano's house. I smiled as I pulled up and saw his family sitting on the front porch. His wife, three kids, aunt, sister, and brother in-law. They were a tight-knit family and they all lived in the same house. Stepping out of the car, I walked up to the porch, and his wife, Lonnie, got up from her chair and hugged me.

"You're back." She smiled. "Look at you. It's been what? Two years since you were here last."

"Yeah." I hugged her tightly.

"I'll go get Ano. He'll be so surprised."

As she went inside to get her husband, I said hello to all his family members. When Ano opened the creaky storm door, he stopped when he saw me.

"Jillian." He held out his arms.

"Hi, Ano."

"It's good to see you again, girl. What's been going on in that humdrum life of yours?"

I took in a deep breath. "I was supposed to get married yesterday."

Ano looked at me and cocked his head. "And you bailed, didn't you?"

"Yep. I sure did."

"Good for you. You know I never liked that little weasel. Come inside and I'll make us some herbal tea."

"I'll make it, dear," Lonnie spoke. "The two of you go sit down and talk."

He led me out the patio door, and we took seats in the lounge chairs that faced the water.

"So, you finally decided it was time to go find yourself."

"Yeah. Pretty much. I just walked away from the only life I'd ever known."

"How does it feel?"

"It feels great, but also a little scary."

"Are you questioning yourself for leaving?"

"No. I've never been so sure of anything in my life."

"Good. It'll make your journey a little easier. But I will warn you, Jillian, in order to continue on with your journey, you need to become fearless of what you may discover and how your life will change."

"I know. I understand that." I looked down.

"What you find out about yourself will be with you forever and there will be no escaping it."

"Here you are," Lonnie spoke as she handed us our tea.

"Thank you, Lonnie." I smiled.

"Thank you, my love." Ano took hold of his wife's hand and kissed it.

They had the kind of relationship that I'd always dreamed of. Every time I visited them growing up, their bond seemed stronger. They had the kind of love that was rare. Unlike my parents, who were at each other's throats 24/7.

"You two are really something special." I smiled at Ano.

He reached over and placed his hand on mine. "You, my friend, will have a love like ours someday."

"I hope so." A small smile crossed my lips.

"You will. You're a beautiful woman with a beautiful soul. I want you to remember one thing."

"What's that?"

"Your journey won't be complete until you make peace with those who love you."

"I can never go back there, Ano." I looked at the water.

"You can and you will. You say that now, but once you get further along and become more aware of who you truly are, you'll know it's the right thing to do. You've come a long way since the day I found you hiding in that cave when you were just ten years old, but this time, I'm not convincing you to go back. That's something you need to do on your own and on your own terms. You'll know when the time is right. Sometimes you need to get lost to be found."

After having dinner with the family, it was time for me to head back to the hotel. As I was in my suite, pouring a glass of wine, there was a knock on the door. When I opened it, I was surprised to see Drew standing there.

"Hi."

"Hi." He smiled.

"Come on in."

As soon as he stepped through the door, I looked down the hall.

"What are you doing?" he asked.

"Where's Jess?"

"She's up in the room. I saw you come back to the hotel and I wanted to talk to you for a minute."

"Oh. Okay. What's up? Do you want some wine?" I asked as I picked up my glass.

"No, thank you. If by chance you run into me and Jess, could you please not mention that we ran into each other today and the whole paddle board thing?"

"Why?" I asked with a twisted face.

Drew placed his hands in his pockets. "She's a very jealous person and she would take it the wrong way."

"Sure. I won't mention it."

"Thanks. I appreciate it."

"No problem." I grinned.

Removing his hand from his pocket, he rubbed the back of his neck.

"I should get going."

"Enjoy the rest of your evening," I spoke.

"You too." Walking to the door, he stopped and turned around. "Did you have a nice visit with your friend?"

"I did. Thanks for asking."

He gave me a small smile as he opened the door and walked out. I stood there, biting down on my bottom lip. He seemed stressed. Maybe I was imaging things. No. He had a stressed look on his face and it made me wonder what was going on.

Chapter Eight
Jillian

I took the elevator down to the restaurant to have breakfast before I started my day. I felt great today. I slept like a baby all night for the first time in years. As the hostess was taking me to my table, I saw Drew and Jess. I pretended not to notice them, but she called me out as I walked by.

"Jillian."

I stopped and plastered on my perfected smile. "Good morning," I spoke.

"Good morning." Drew gave a small smile.

"Do you have dinner plans for tonight?" Jess asked.

Shit. Really? Oh God, no. I started to fumble with my words and just thought to hell with it. She'd know I was lying.

"No. Actually, I don't."

"Excellent. Drew and I would love for you to join us. Right, baby?" she asked as she placed her hand on his.

"Sure." He looked down.

"I would hate to impose on your vacation," I spoke.

"You wouldn't be imposing at all. If I thought that, I wouldn't have asked. So, yes?"

"Yes. That would be nice. Thank you."

"Great. I'll have Drew make reservations and then we'll pick you up at your room, say around seven o'clock?"

"Seven sounds good."

"Which room are you in?" she asked as she cocked her head.

"The Presidential Suite on the ninth floor."

"Perfect. We'll see you at seven."

"Enjoy your day." I smiled as I walked away.

My mind went back to what Drew said to me last night about her being a jealous person. Why would she invite me to have dinner with them? She knew Drew and I met on the plane and I could tell by her reaction when we first met that she instantly hated me. Why the sudden change of heart? I sighed as I sipped my coffee. Now that I thought more about it, Drew never looked happy when I saw the two of them together, and it was like he was a different person when he was with her. It was almost as if he was a different man than the one I met on the plane and paddle boarded with yesterday.

When I headed out to the private boat I rented, Juno was there to greet me.

"It's nice to see you again, Jillian." He smiled as he hugged me.

"It's good to see you too."

"Are you alone this trip?"

"Yeah. I've decided to embark on a journey of self-discovery."

"Self-discovery is good." He smiled as he handed me some scuba gear. "And what better way to get in touch with yourself than to swim with the dolphins? I'm going to take you to a special place not many of us take visitors. But for you, I'll take you there."

Juno started the boat and took me to a cove. As I stood there, looking over the side of the boat, I saw a group of dolphins swimming around the crystal clear, aqua blue water. I would never grow tired of this. I'd been swimming with the dolphins for years and loved every minute of it, but this time, it would be a different experience for me.

"There they are. They're waiting for you to play with them, Jillian." Juno smiled.

As soon as I climbed into the water, a group of dolphins swam up to me as my hands skimmed the top of the water. I'd learned over the years how to play with them by swimming around in a circle. Suddenly, they started to swim away and then circled back, with one of them brushing his nose against my body as if to tell me to follow them. Diving down into the water, I followed them out a few feet and found myself in pure bliss. They were in a playful mood. Some were spinning around me while others were jumping out of the water. They welcomed me into their oceanic playground. They kept a close eye on me as if they knew what I was going through and every emotion that flooded my mind. I found myself in the presence of joy and peacefulness. I was suddenly face to face with one dolphin as he was mere millimeters from me. I slowly brought up my hands and placed them on each side of his nose. As I stared into his eyes, I became aware of this moment. As if I suddenly woke up from a life that had only been a dream. I saw freedom and fearlessness. His clicking became more pronounced and the other dolphins swam over to me. I found myself encircled by them, and as I looked around into each of their eyes, I felt an abundance of love and strength.

Returning to the surface of the water, I played with them for a while longer and then climbed back into the boat.

"Magical, wasn't it?" Juno smiled.

"Beyond magical, Juno."

As I stared over the side of the boat one last time before Juno took me back, the dolphins jumped up out of the water and spun around. Two of them came to the side of the boat and stared up at me as I ran my hand along their noses.

"Thank you," I spoke to them.

Turning around and diving back into the water, they disappeared, but the feeling that I got from our time together never would.

****

Passing by one of the shops in the hotel, a dress in the window caught my eye. It was a strapless, red floral print wraparound that would be perfect for dinner tonight with Drew and Jess. Walking into the shop, I asked the saleswoman if I could see it.

"What size are you?" she asked.

"Size 4."

She smiled as she took the dress off the mannequin and handed it to me.

"Perfect. It's your size and the only one we got in. I would say that you are meant to wear it. Would you like to try it on?"

"Yes. Please."

As I stood and stared at myself in the full-length mirror, I ran my hands down my sides. The dress fit perfectly and I was in love with it. After making my purchase, I headed back up to my suite, showered, and got ready for dinner, which somehow I felt was going to be awkward at its best.

Just as I put the final touches on my makeup, there was a knock at the door. My belly started to do tiny flips and I wasn't sure why. I had nothing to be nervous about. I was just having dinner with a man I met on the plane and his girlfriend. Opening the door, my eyes instantly diverted their attention to Drew. Good lord, was he hot. A number of things took over me, one being the ache between my legs and the thought of how I needed to take care of that later.

"Love that dress," Jess spoke as she looked me up and down.

"Thank you. You look so pretty." I smiled.

"Thanks. Are you ready? The car is waiting for us downstairs."

"Hello, Jillian." Drew nodded.

"Hi." I gave a small and careful smile as not to upset the girlfriend.

I grabbed my purse and we headed out of the hotel.

****

Drew

My heart picked up the pace the minute Jillian opened the door. My God, she was so beautiful. I loved the way her long brown, blonde-highlighted hair with the subtle waves swept over her shoulders. Her lips were stained in a perfect red color that matched her dress, which hugged her body in all the right places. Jess and I had had a small argument before leaving the room. It wasn't anything major, just her complaining that she felt I wasn't being romantic on this trip, and it was enough to set me off for the rest of the night. I couldn't take my eyes off Jillian and I needed to be careful because my cock was being uncooperative.

As soon as we were seated at a cabana table at Azure, I ordered a double scotch. I was going to need it to get through this night with a woman of whom I had already had enough and a woman for whom I was pretty sure I was falling head over heels for. Fuck my life.

"Aren't you going to order us a bottle of champagne, Drew?" Jess asked with a slight attitude.

"If you want a bottle of champagne, then I will order one."

"I'm fine with my fruity drink." Jillian held up her cocktail glass with a smile.

That smile. It was something that took my breath away every time she did it.

When the waitress came back to our table, she took our order, and I asked her to bring a bottle of their finest champagne, just to shut Jess up. I was fine with my scotch and Jillian was happy with her fruity cocktail.

"How was your day?" Jess asked her.

"It was wonderful. I swam with the dolphins."

"Oh. You actually got in the water with those creatures? I could never."

"It was a lot of fun."

"They're so slimy." Jess shuddered.

Jillian casually picked up her drink and took a sip without responding.

"I think swimming with the dolphins sounds like fun." I smiled at Jillian.

"You would, Drew. I don't think I would allow you to sleep in my bed after being in the water with those things."

Rolling my eyes, I thought to myself, *I think I'll go tomorrow.*

Chapter Nine
Jillian

I was starting to understand the unhappiness that radiated from Drew when he was with Jess. She was definitely a piece of work. She reminded me of Grant and that was not a good thing.

"So, Jillian, what made you decide to leave your fiancé standing at the altar?" she asked.

"Don't you think that's a little personal?" Drew interjected.

"No. She told you that she did it, so I was just wondering why."

Sitting there, I was feeling uncomfortable about her question, but I wasn't going to let her get to me. If she wanted to know, then I would tell her.

"I wasn't in love with him."

"Fair enough. But didn't you know that before the wedding?"

I wasn't about to get into my whole life story with this bitch I didn't even know.

"I had my doubts, but when I found out that he slept with two strippers at his bachelor party, that sealed the deal," I lied.

"Oh you poor thing. I wouldn't have left him at the altar. I would have castrated him first and then left him." She reached over and placed her arm around Drew. "That's something I never have to worry about with Drew. Right, baby?" She leaned over and kissed his cheek.

He nodded his head as he gulped down the rest of his scotch and the waitress quickly brought him another.

"What do you do for a living?" I asked her.

"I'm a buyer for Neiman Marcus. And you?"

"I just graduated from Yale Law."

Her brow raised and, suddenly, I became a threat.

"Wow. Impressive. I never would have taken you for the lawyer type."

Her and me both.

"How long have the two of you been together?" I asked.

"About a year now." She smiled. "A wonderful and beautiful year. Isn't that right, baby?" She smiled.

Drew raised his brows as he took another sip of his drink. It was taking everything I had to hold in the laughter that so desperately wanted to come out. Things were starting to become very clear now. She invited me to have dinner with them so she could tell me how happy they were and to discreetly tell me to stay away.

"That's great. I'm in a man-free zone and I couldn't be happier." I smiled.

"Really?" she asked with a twisted face.

"Yes. I'm on a journey of self-discovery and I have rid men from my life. No exceptions."

"Forever?"

"No. Not forever. But I don't have any plans to be involved with a man in the near future. I need to find myself first."

All of a sudden, her attitude changed towards me.

"That is wonderful, Jillian. You are very inspiring. If I didn't already know who I was, I'd go on a little journey myself." She winked as she sipped her champagne. "If you'll excuse me, I need to use the little girls' room."

As soon as she left, Drew looked at me and started shaking his head.

"I'm sorry about her asking you about your fiancé. Sometimes she has no filter or regard for other people's feelings. Actually, make that all the time." He smiled.

"No big deal." I waved my hand in front of my face.

"Well, just so you know, it was a big deal to me."

"So what did you two talk about when I was gone?" Jess asked as she sat down.

"I was just asking Jillian about the dolphins," Drew replied.

"Are you still on that, baby? We aren't going to swim with them."

Drew sighed and picked up his drink. I could tell he was getting very angry by the way he clenched his jaw. After finishing our dinner and having a light conversation, it was getting late, so we headed back to the hotel.

"Thank you again for inviting me to dinner. I had a nice time." I smiled at both of them.

"Thank you for joining us," Drew spoke.

"Yes. We must do this again on our last night here," Jess said.

"I'm looking forward to it. Have a nice night." I smiled as I stepped off the elevator.

****

Drew

A few days had passed and Jess and I weren't getting along at all. Everything that came out of her mouth annoyed me. All she did was whine and complain about everything. Mostly about me. After doing some shopping, she huffed and puffed all the way back to the hotel because I wouldn't buy her a bracelet she wanted.

"You haven't bought me one single thing since we got here," she spoke in a harsh tone.

I could feel my blood boiling as I opened the door to the suite.

"What about all the meals I've bought you?" I yelled. "The plane tickets, this suite, the bottles of champagne you had to have every night, and the tickets for everything you wanted to do!"

"Don't you dare take that tone with me, Drew. All I want is for you to buy me something nice. That's what boyfriends are supposed to do. When you love someone, you buy them nice things. Is that so much to ask?"

The rage that had been contained inside me began to erupt and I couldn't take it anymore. Just the mere sound of her voice sent me over the edge.

"I DON'T LOVE YOU!" I shouted. "I can't do this anymore, Jess."

"What?" Tears started to fill her eyes.

"I'm sorry, but it's over between us," I softly spoke.

"Don't say that, baby. You don't mean it," she begged.

"Yes I do. It's been over for a while now. We haven't been getting along and everything's always my fault. I've had enough."

The tears began to stream down her face and, sadly, I didn't give a damn. She had pushed me way too far.

"You heartless bastard. How could you do this to me? I love you, you son of a bitch." She grabbed hold of my arm.

Jerking it away, I looked into her eyes. "Of course it's my fault this happened. Well, let me give you a wake-up call, darling. You are a whiney, jealous, self-righteous, selfish, stuck-up bitch, and god help the next man that crosses your path."

She raised her hand and slapped me across the face. "How dare you speak to me like that."

I held my face to try and soothe the sting of the burn. "Pack your stuff and leave," I shouted as I pulled out my phone. "There's a four o'clock flight back to New York and you need to be on it."

"I'm not going anywhere. You leave. You're the one who broke up with me, you fucking asshole," she screamed.

I walked into the bedroom and threw her suitcase on the bed. As I was grabbing her clothes from the drawers, she grabbed my arm.

"Stop it!" she screamed.

Jerking away from her, I went into the bathroom, collected her things, and threw them into her bag.

"This is my room, that I paid for. I'm not going anywhere. Now get out before I call security and have you thrown out!" I yelled as I pointed to the door.

"You'll regret this, Drew Westbrook!"

I grabbed her suitcase and carry-on bag, opened the door, and set them in the hallway.

"The only thing I regret is not doing this sooner."

As soon as she stepped out of the suite, I slammed the door.

****

Jillian

I had a great time with Ano and Lonnie at the luau they invited me to, and by time I got back to the hotel, it was eleven o'clock. When I approached the elevators, there was a sign that they were out of order.

"I'm sorry, miss. You'll have to use the elevators around the corner and across from the bar.

"Okay, thank you."

As I walked around the corner, I pushed the button and waited for the elevator to come down. While I was waiting, I glanced across at the bar that was filled with people and noticed Drew sitting on one of the barstools. I hadn't seen him or Jess the past couple of days, so I thought I'd stop over and say hi.

"Hey," I spoke as I walked up to him.

"Jillian Bell. Can I buy you a drink?" he slurred.

"No thanks." I narrowed my eye at him. "Where's Jess?"

"I broke it off with her and sent her home." He kicked back his drink, finishing it off.

"I'm sorry to hear that." I didn't know what to say and I was shocked.

"Don't be. I'm not. I should have done it a long time ago. Bartender?" He held up his finger.

"No you don't. I think you've had enough to drink. Come on." I grabbed hold of his arm. "Let's get you back to your room."

He didn't resist as I hooked his arm around my neck and took him up to his suite.

"Where's your keycard?" I asked as I propped him up against the wall.

He reached in his pocket. "I think I left it in the room," he slurred.

"Are you sure?"

"It's not in my pockets."

"Okay. Come on, back on the elevator." I sighed as I hooked his arm around my neck.

"Where are we going?" He stumbled and almost fell.

"To my room so I can call the front desk and get you another key."

Stumbling down the hallway, I propped Drew up so I could get the key from my purse. The moment I let go of him, he slid down the wall and to the ground.

"Ugh. Come on, big guy." I helped him back up and took him to the bedroom.

"We have something in common," he spoke. "Something I think you should know."

"Oh yeah. What's that?" I asked as I helped him onto the bed.

"We both left someone standing at the altar."

Did I just hear him right?

"What?" I frowned as I stared down at him.

"I left my fiancée at the altar just like you did." He rolled over.

I knew trying to find out more was going to be impossible in the condition he was in. He probably wouldn't even remember that he told me in the morning. Picking up the phone on the nightstand, I dialed the front desk.

"Front desk, how may I help you."

Looking at Drew, I saw that he had fallen sound asleep.

"I'm sorry. I've changed my mind." I hung up.

There was no use in trying to get him back to his room. He'd most likely be out the rest of night anyway. After removing his shoes and socks, I covered him with a blanket. Grabbing my nightshirt, I took it to the second bedroom, slipped into it, and climbed into bed. Why didn't he tell me that he could relate after I told him about Grant? And this whole thing with Jess. Wow. I could tell he was unhappy, so I was not totally surprised. Something really bad must have happened for him to do it on vacation and send her home. Which led me to another question. Where was home for him? I never did ask.

Chapter Ten
Drew

My head felt like someone had taken a hammer to it as I struggled to open my eyes. Where was I? This wasn't my room. Shit. I placed my hand on my forehead. I was fully clothed except my shoes and socks were off. Slowly climbing out of bed, I walked into the living area of the suite and saw Jillian sitting at the table.

"Uh, hey," I spoke as I rubbed the back of my neck.

"Good morning." She smiled brightly. "How are you feeling?"

"Like shit. Um, how did I end up here?" I asked as I walked over to the table and took a seat.

"You don't remember?"

"No. I don't."

"I saw you at the bar last night and I helped you to your room, but when we got there, you didn't have your key, so I brought you back here. I was going to call the front desk to have them bring an extra key, but the minute you hit the bed, you were out. So, I just let you sleep."

"And where did you sleep?"

"In the other bedroom."

Suddenly, there was knock on the door.

"Are you expecting someone?" I asked.

"Room service. I ordered us breakfast. I figured you'd need some coffee the minute you woke up."

"Thanks. I appreciate it."

"I can take it from here," Jillian spoke as she wheeled the rolling cart over to the table.

She picked up the pot of coffee and poured some into a cup.

"Here. Drink away." She smiled.

"I'm sorry about last night. Thank you for taking care of me, but you should have just left my dumb ass down there."

"Why? And don't be sorry. It happens to all of us. I'm sorry about Jess. Do you want to talk about it?" she asked as she removed the silver lids from the plates.

"No. Not really." I took a sip of coffee. "I'd had enough. It was something I should have done months ago."

"If you were so unhappy, why didn't you?" she asked innocently.

I cocked my head and raised my brow. "Really?"

She held up her finger and smirked. "Right."

I gave her a small smile as I continued to drink my coffee and attempted to eat some eggs. When I finished eating and finished up my third cup of coffee, I got up from my seat.

"Thank you for letting me crash here last night and thank you for breakfast. I better head back to my room and shower. I still reek of alcohol."

"Yeah, you do." She wrinkled her nose.

I chuckled. "I guess I'm going to have to go down to the front desk and get another key."

"Don't forget your shoes and socks." She smiled.

"Ah, yes. I mustn't forget those."

Walking into the bedroom, I put on my socks and shoes and then headed towards the door.

"Enjoy your day, Jillian," I spoke before heading out.

"You too, Drew."

After getting a new key to the suite, I stepped into the shower and let the hot water stream down my body. I couldn't believe I got so drunk last night. That wasn't my intention. All I could think about while I was at the bar was Jillian and how much I really liked her. The conversation from dinner the other night kept playing over and over in my mind and how she told us that she had rid men from her life. Now that I was single, there would be no way I could have a chance with her. She made it very clear that she was living in a man-free zone and that was something I would respect. I didn't even know where her next destination was after Hawaii and the thought of her traveling alone bothered me.

Stepping out of the shower, I wrapped a towel around my waist, checked my phone, and noticed there were six text messages from Jess.

"How could you do this to us?"

"I love you. I'm sorry."

"I promise I'll change. Please give me another chance."

"Please, Drew."

"I forgive you for the things you said to me."

"I love you. Please."

Sighing, I pulled up her contact info and blocked her. I had a feeling she was going to be a problem when I got back to New York. Thank God I never let her keep any of her things at my place.

****

Jillian

There was a part of me that couldn't stop thinking about Drew. I had gotten the impression he did everything Jess wanted to do and nothing he wanted to. He made a comment at dinner the other night about swimming with the dolphins and I could tell that he really wanted to do it, so I had a thought. Changing into my bikini and throwing my hair up in a ponytail, I slipped on my cover-up and went up to Drew's suite.

"Hey." He smiled as he opened the door. "Come on in."

I got up close to him and took a whiff of his body.

"What are you doing?" He laughed.

"Making sure you smell clean and free of alcohol."

"Did I pass?"

"Yep. With flying colors." I smiled. "Anyway, go put on your swim trunks."

"Why?" He narrowed his eye.

"Because we're going to go swim with the dolphins."

"Seriously?" His grin grew wide.

"Seriously. Now get a move on because Juno is waiting for us."

"Who's Juno?" I asked as I walked to the bedroom.

"Our captain."

We hopped into my rental car and I drove us to where Juno was waiting for us with his boat.

"Why are you doing this?" Drew asked.

"Doing what?"

"Taking me to swim with the dolphins."

"I kind of got the impression that since you've been here, you have done everything Jess wanted to do and nothing you wanted to. At dinner the other night, you seemed really interested in swimming with the dolphins and she just kind of dismissed you. So I thought you should get the chance to do it while you're here." I looked over at him.

"That's really nice of you. Again, thank you." He placed his hand on my arm, and suddenly, I felt like I couldn't breathe.

"Just paying it forward and making your shitty time here a little less shitty." I grinned.

"I appreciate it." He laughed.

Drew

Swimming with the dolphins was the highlight of my entire trip. I had never experienced anything like it or the sense of peace that inhabited me. When we were finished, we headed back to the hotel.

"That was—"

"Magical?" Jillian smiled as she glanced over at me.

"Yes. Very magical. Listen, I was thinking. I want to thank you for such a great day, so I was hoping you'd agree to have dinner tonight."

"You don't have to take me to dinner, Drew."

"I know I don't. I want to." I smiled. "I'm leaving tomorrow morning, so I thought one last dinner would be nice."

The grin on her face widened. "Okay. Dinner it is. Just give me some time to shower and get ready."

"How about I pick you up at six o'clock?"

"Six will be good."

Walking into my suite, I headed to the bathroom and turned on the water for a shower. Spending the day with her was amazing and the things I'd felt for her before only intensified. Being with her and in her presence made me a happy man. I hadn't felt this way in a very long time, if ever. Leaving tomorrow morning was going to be hard because I'd probably never see her again. It didn't matter anyway; she was on a journey to find herself and I wasn't going to stand in the way of that. For tonight, I would enjoy the next few hours spent with her and then tomorrow, it was back to reality with only the memory of a girl I met on a plane who enriched my life in such a short period of time.

Chapter Eleven
Jillian

Stepping out of the shower and slipping into my robe, I facetimed Kellan.

"Hey, you. How's it going in Hawaii?"

"It's great. How are you?" I asked as I started to put on my makeup.

"I'm good. No complaints. Are you going somewhere?"

"Yeah." I smiled as I looked at my phone. "I'm having dinner with Drew."

"You're having dinner with the guy from the plane and his girlfriend?"

"Nope. Just him. He broke up with her and kicked her out."

"Jilly Bean, I thought you were in a man-free zone?"

"I am. It's a goodbye dinner. He's leaving tomorrow and so am I. No big deal."

"He broke up with her in Hawaii? Wow."

"I know, but he was very unhappy. She was kind of a bitch."

"So let me get this straight. He broke up with his girlfriend, while on vacation, may I add, you broke it off with Grant, and now the two of you are single and having dinner together. Sounds like a rebound to me."

"Ugh, Kellan. It's dinner. It's not like I'm sleeping with him. He's my friend."

"Where does he live?"

"I don't know. I never asked."

"Why? Don't friends usually ask each other where they live?"

"Does it matter? It's not like I'll ever see him again."

"True."

"I'm hanging up now, Kel. I'll call you when I get to New York."

"Sounds good, Bean. Have a good night with Airplane Guy and have a safe flight."

"Thanks. I'll talk to you soon."

After ending the call, I blow dried my hair, sprayed it, and slipped into a long black floral print maxi dress. The truth was that I felt something for Drew. He was an amazing man with a good heart. He was also a man that I could see myself falling madly in love with. Meeting him couldn't have happened at a worse time.

As I slipped on my shoes, there was a knock at the door. When I opened it, I swallowed hard when I saw Drew, face of the gods, standing there in his khaki-colored casual pants and a white button-down shirt with the sleeves rolled up. *Shit*. My lady parts were on fire.

"Hi there." I smiled.

"You look gorgeous." He winked.

"Thanks. You're looking pretty hot yourself there, Mr. Westbrook."

"Are you ready to go?" He held out his arm.

"I am." I smiled as I hooked my arm around his.

We climbed into my rental car and Drew drove us to a place called Hau Tree Lanai where we were seated outside beneath an arching Hau tree by the ocean and he ordered us a bottle of wine.

"Tell me more about you," he spoke.

"Well, I grew up very wealthy with parents who controlled everything I did, right down to the food I put in my mouth. They tried to mold me into the perfect daughter. I could have no flaws. After so many years of molding, I became exactly who they wanted me to be. I wasn't allowed to make any decisions for myself and that is why I don't know who I am." I picked up my glass and took a sip of wine.

"I'm sorry. I couldn't imagine growing up like that."

"So tell me about your parents." I smiled as I set my glass down.

"My dad was a construction worker until he got injured on the job and had to go on disability, and my mom is a nurse. Things were tight growing up, but I had everything I needed. My parents are great people and we're very close."

I gave him a small smile. "That's how a family should be. So how did you get the funds to start your own technology company?"

"I'd always been interested in technology since I could remember. You could say I was a bit of a geek." He smirked. "You know the 'Cloud'?"

"Yeah." I narrowed my eye at him.

"I developed it when I studied at MIT."

"SHUT UP!" I exclaimed as I slightly leaned across the table.

Drew chuckled. "It's true. I developed it and sold it for a fuck ton of money. I paid off all of my parent's debt, bought them a new house, made a nice deposit in their bank account, and opened my own company."

"How old were you?"

"Twenty when I sold Cloud and twenty-one when I opened the doors to Westbrook Technology, Inc."

"Did you graduate from MIT?" I asked.

"Yes. I graduated when I was twenty-one. I graduated high school earlier than most kids."

"So you're a genius?" I smiled.

"Nah, not really. I'm just smart, I guess."

"Oh please. You're a freaking genius and don't be ashamed to admit it." I held up my glass to him.

"Touché, Miss Bell. I would say the same about you graduating top in your class at Yale Law." His glass touched mine.

I gave him a small smile as I took a sip. The one thing that I was dying to know about him was why he left his fiancée. It was so bizarre to me that I met someone who did the same thing I had done. Should I ask him? Would it be too personal? I told him about why I did it so I thought that it was only fair he told me.

"I have something I want to ask you, and to be honest, it's been bothering me."

"What is it?" He cocked his head.

"Just before you passed out last night, you told me that we had something in common. You said that you left your fiancée on your wedding day."

He leaned back in his chair as his eyes burned into mine.

"I told you that, eh?"

"Yeah. You did." I nodded. "I just wondered why. I mean, you can tell me that it's none of my business, but remember, I spilled my guts to you."

"True." He took in a deep breath. "I did leave my fiancée on our wedding day. I had just sold Cloud and made millions, graduated from MIT, and I guess I figured why the hell not? I met Marley at MIT and we had been together for a little over a year. It just seemed to make sense for some reason. She did all the planning and I just agreed to everything, but I was having doubts during the process. When our wedding day came, I just couldn't see myself or a future with her. Or anyone, for that matter. It just doesn't seem natural to spend the rest of your life with someone."

"But your parents."

"I know. They have a great relationship, and as much as I admire them, I just couldn't see myself like that. So, before the ceremony, I mustered up the courage to go into the room she was waiting in and I told her that I couldn't do it."

"She must have been heartbroken."

"She was. She cried like I never saw her cry before, called me all kinds of names, and told me to get the hell out. So I did and I never looked back. It was probably the hardest thing I ever did, but it was for the best. She's married now with two kids and she's happy."

"Weird how life works out sometimes. So you never see yourself getting married and having a family?"

"Nah. Not really. I guess it's who I am."

"Well, at least you know who you are." I smiled.

After finishing dinner, we took a walk along the shoreline. Taking off my shoes and throwing them into the sand, I lifted up my dress so the bottom didn't get all wet. Drew took off his shoes and socks and rolled up the bottom of his pants. Darkness had settled in and the moon shined above us, lighting our path as the gentle tide swept across our feet.

"Thank you for dinner," I spoke as I nudged his shoulder with mine.

"You're welcome. It was my pleasure." He looked over at me.

Something stirred inside me. My belly flipped and my heart started to pick up its pace. I stopped and he stopped alongside me and placed his hand on my cheek.

"You are so beautiful, Jillian. Both inside and out," he spoke as his head dipped closer to mine.

I gulped.

"Thank you, Drew." I stared into his dark eyes.

He swallowed hard and removed his hand from my cheek.

"We better head back. It's getting late."

Chapter Twelve
Drew

The connection I felt with her was unlike anything I'd ever felt before. I wanted to kiss her, but I had to refrain because if I did, I didn't know if I'd ever be able to say goodbye. I knew that once my lips touched hers, it would be something that would haunt me for the rest of my life. As we approached her suite, she asked me to come inside for one last drink before I left. Was that a good idea? Probably not, especially with the way I felt about her, but any last moment I could spend with her was gold and I wasn't about to turn it down.

"Let me pour." I smiled as I took the bottle of wine from her.

Handing her a glass, we took a seat in the chairs out on the balcony and listened to the subtle waves hit the shore.

"I'm sure going to miss it here," she spoke.

"Me too."

It was killing me not to know where she was headed to next. But for both our sakes, it was best that I didn't. Looking over at her, I noticed she had something in her hair. As I reached over to get it, she reached up and placed her hand on mine.

"Sorry, but you had something in your hair."

"Thanks." Her eyes gazed into mine.

"I should get going," I spoke as I got up from my chair.

"Okay." She followed me to the door.

Turning around, my heart felt heavy as I struggled to say goodbye.

"Thank you again for making my time here a little less shitty." I smiled as I took hold of her hand and brought it up to my lips.

"You're welcome. It was fun." She grinned.

Fuck. The desire to kiss her was burning inside me. Before I left, I had to know what her lips felt like. If I didn't, I'd spend my whole life regretting it. Just a small kiss wouldn't hurt. A friendly kiss would be all. Nothing deep, nothing heavy. As our eyes stayed fixated on each other, I brought my hand up to her face and slowly lowered my head as my lips softly brushed against hers. I waited for her to pull away, but she didn't. She welcomed it and kissed me back. I needed to go, but I couldn't tear myself away from her. One kiss turned into two and then three. I looked at her as I pushed a strand of her hair behind her ear, waiting, making sure that it was okay. She reached up and her lips once again collided with mine. This time, our tongues met and greeted each other with warmth. My cock was on the rise as the heat was on my skin. My hands roamed up and down the sides of her hourglass figure and a soft moan escaped her. Her hands left my face and started unbuttoning my shirt. She wanted me just as bad as I wanted her. As she slid my shirt off my shoulders, I untied the ties of her dress and let it fall to the ground, and she stood there almost naked with only her panties covering her. Picking her up, I carried her to the bedroom and softly laid her on the bed, hovering over her while my mouth explored her beautiful round breasts and my fingers traveled down the edge of her panties. Her moans were music to my ears as I dipped my finger inside her, taking in the wetness that surrounded her.

"You're so wet and you feel so good," I moaned.

"So do you." She arched her back, forcing my fingers to deepen inside her.

A few more strokes and soft circles around her clit, she let out the most pleasing sound as she orgasmed. Standing up, I kicked off my shoes and took down my pants, setting free my rock hard cock that was ready to explode. Spreading her legs, I kissed up her inner thigh as she threw her head back in delight while my tongue slid its way up to her outer lips. Taking in the sweet taste of her, I placed my hands firmly on her hips as my lips wrapped around her clit, lightly sucking until she couldn't take anymore. Her hands ran through my hair as her body tightened and another orgasm took her over.

****

Jillian

My body was on fire with passion, a feeling I'd never experienced before. This man and his mouth had me in such a state that left my insides screaming for more. The way his tongue caressed my most sensitive area floored me.

"I don't have any condoms on me. They're in my room," he spoke with bated breath as he looked up at me.

"I'm on birth control, so you don't have to worry. I trust you, Drew."

His mouth explored my abdomen and my breasts. The way his lips wrapped around my hardened nipples excited me, as did the feel of his perfectly sized hard cock rubbing against my inner thigh. Hovering over me, he gently thrust into me until his entire length was buried deep inside. A moan escaped his lips as our eyes locked onto each other's while he tenderly moved in and out of me. I swelled around him and he felt it. His pleasurable moans told me all as did mine to him. My nails dug into his back as his lips met mine and his thrusting became faster, sending me over the edge and into my third orgasm of the night.

"Yes. That's it, come with me." He strained, filling me up with his come.

Collapsing on top of me, he interlaced our fingers, brought my arms over my head, and stared into my eyes while we each tried to catch our breath. Once our heart rates returned to normal, he lifted himself up and pulled out of me. As we rolled onto our sides, he ran his finger across my cheek with a smile.

"You were incredible."

"So were you." I smiled back.

"Do you want me to leave or do you want me to stay the night?"

"I want you to stay. That way, I can say goodbye in the morning."

His lips gently brushed against mine before we climbed under the covers and I snuggled against him.

This wasn't supposed to happen. Did I regret it? No. Not in the least. Come tomorrow, we'd part ways with only the memory of this night and the journey I was on would continue. I wrapped my leg around him as his strong muscular arms held me. Grant rarely held me after sex and it was something I was used to. But this. Being wrapped around Drew's body was something I liked. I felt secure and safe in his arms. Something I never knew I desperately needed.

The next morning, when Drew's alarm on his phone went off, his arms tightened around me.

"Good morning," I spoke as I looked up at him.

"Good morning. I need to go. I have to get packed and head to the airport."

"I know."

"Hand me your phone," he spoke.

Reaching over to the nightstand, I grabbed my phone and handed it to him.

"There. You have my number. If you ever need anything or need help, please call me. I can be wherever you are in a flash."

"Thanks. But I'll be okay."

"I know you will be. But you have it just in case." He kissed the top of my head and climbed out of bed.

After he got dressed, I walked him to the door.

"I had a great time last night." He smiled as his hand swept over my hair.

"I did too."

"Good luck on your journey. I hope you find yourself and the happiness you deserve."

Taking hold of his hand, I pressed his palm against my lips.

"Good bye, Drew."

"Good bye, Jillian." His lips softly kissed mine and he walked out the door.

Suddenly, it felt like all the air had left me and I couldn't breathe. Sinking down to the ground, I brought my knees up to my chest and tightly wrapped my arms around them. Tears started streaming down my face and I didn't know why. Confusion set in and, suddenly, I was afraid. Picking myself up off the floor, I took a shower, dressed, and headed to Ano's house to say goodbye. When I arrived, all he needed was to take one look at me to know something was wrong.

"You've come to say goodbye, Jillian, but you seem so sad."

"I messed up, Ano. I slept with someone last night and it wreaked havoc on my emotional well-being."

"The man from the plane?" he asked as we sat down.

"Yes. He left today to go back to wherever he calls home and the minute he left, I started sobbing."

"Do you know why?"

"I don't know; that's the thing."

"Do you have feelings for this man?" he asked as he placed his hands on mine.

"Yes, no. I don't know. All I know is that when he held me, for the first time in my life, I felt safe."

"Ah." He slowly nodded his head. "You discovered that you need safety."

"But I always thought I felt safe."

"Your perception of safe and the reality of it are two different things. It's natural for a child to feel safe in the company of their parents because they are supposed to protect us. It wasn't until you shared a special connection with that man that you realized you never felt it. Remember what I told you about your journey. You need to be fearless because every road you travel on will bring something about yourself that you didn't know or realize. Now it's up to you to take what you realized and find safety within yourself."

"How?"

"You'll figure it out along the way. You're a strong and smart woman. Don't underestimate your strengths."

I got up from my chair and gave him a hug.

"Thank you, Ano. I better get going. I still have to pack and get to the airport."

"Take care, my child. Don't be a stranger."

I gave him a smile as I kissed his cheek.

"I won't be."

Heading back to the hotel, I gave a lot of thought about what Ano said. My whole life had been spent being around people who controlled me, and now that I was alone, what I thought I knew I didn't really know at all.

Chapter Thirteen
Drew

"Thanks, Randall. I'll see you in the morning," I spoke as I climbed out of the Bentley.

Walking up the steps of my townhouse, I saw my next door neighbor and friend, Liam Wyatt.

"Hey, you're back. How was Hawaii?" he asked.

"It was eventful." I smirked.

"In a bad way or a good way?"

"Both. I broke up with Jess and made her leave early."

"Oh. I'm sorry to hear that."

I gave him a small smile. "No you're not. You never liked her."

He shrugged. "True. But still. You're better off without her. She reminded me too much of Oliver's ex."

"Yeah. I should have listened to you on that one. Stop by this week and we'll have a drink."

"Sure will, Drew. Welcome home." He waved.

Stepping into the house, I took my suitcase upstairs and then headed to the kitchen for something to eat. I smiled when I opened the refrigerator and there were a couple of stacked containers sitting there with a note from my housekeeper, Jane.

"Welcome home, Drew. I slaved all day to make these meals, so you better eat them."

Taking one of the containers out, I threw it in the microwave and walked over to the bar to pour myself a scotch. I already missed her. The moment I walked out of her hotel room, a feeling overcame me. A feeling that something was missing from my life. The time I spent with her on the plane. and the few times in Hawaii, made me feel like a different person, and now, I didn't think I'd ever felt so lonely.

Opening my eyes to the sound of my alarm, I stumbled out of bed, showered, and headed down to the kitchen for some coffee.

"Morning, Jane."

"Good morning, Drew." She smiled as she poured me a cup of coffee. "How was your trip?"

I sighed. "Let's just say that Jess won't be coming over here anymore. I ended things with her."

She made the sign of the cross and then placed her hands together.

"Thank you, lord."

I lightly chuckled. "I know you weren't a fan of hers."

"No. No, I wasn't. What did she do this time?"

"Just her usual shit. She basically told me that I was a bad boyfriend because I wouldn't buy her something."

Jane rolled her eyes. "Well, maybe if she wasn't such a bad girlfriend, you would have bought her what she wanted. You're a good man, Drew. Don't let that little hussy tell you any different."

"Trust me. I'm not giving her a second thought. Thanks for the coffee and now I have to head to the office." I gave her a kiss on the cheek.

"Have a good day."

Jane had worked for me for the last four years. She was a godsend. Not only did I love her, but my parents and friends did as well. She did everything for me and had quickly become a part of my family.

****

"Good morning, Lia," I spoke as I walked past my secretary's desk.

"Welcome back, Drew. How was Hawaii?"

"It was nice. Thank you. If Jess calls, don't put her through. We're over," I spoke as she followed me into my office.

"Oh. Okay. I left some papers on your desk that you need to sign and you have a meeting in thirty minutes to look over the new software proposal."

I sighed. "I know."

"Anything else?" she asked.

"No. That's all."

Taking a seat at my desk, I leaned back in my chair and picked up the papers that needed to be signed. After looking them over, I threw them back down. The only thing on my mind was Jillian and our night together. God, she was by far the best woman I'd ever had sex with. Everything she did aroused me. Her soft moans, her gentle touch, her smell, and the way her body moved with mine was undeniable. How long was this going to last? Me thinking about her non-stop? *Fuck.* I should have asked for her number or at least asked where she was headed to next. I was worried, something I generally didn't do with women. As I was deep in thought, my friend and VP, Lance, walked in.

"Hey, buddy. Welcome back." He smiled.

"Thanks."

"So did you get things resolved with Jess?" he asked as he took a seat across from my desk.

"Actually, I did. I broke up with her and sent her home."

He chuckled. "In Hawaii?"

"Yep."

"Classic and so deserved. It was about time, man. She was toxic."

"But now that I got rid of that problem, I have another."

"What's that?" He leaned back in his chair.

"I met someone and I can't stop thinking about her."

"In Hawaii?"

"Actually, she sat next to me on the plane to Hawaii and we stayed at the same hotel. Jess invited her to dinner one night to try and prove to me that she changed."

"And I can see that worked out really well." He laughed. "So now you have me curious. Who is this mystery girl?"

"Her name is Jillian Bell and she's the most beautiful, fun, kind-hearted, selfless, amazing woman I have ever met."

"Hmm. I've never heard you describe a woman like that before." He rubbed his chin. "Did you fuck her?"

"Yes, but that's not important. What's important is that I don't think I'll ever see her again."

"Why? Where does she live?"

"She lived in Seattle, but she won't go back there. I don't know where she went after she left Hawaii."

"Okay, Drew. Seriously, I'm so confused right now, man."

"She left her fiancé at the altar on her wedding day and hopped on a plane to Hawaii to start a journey of self-discovery."

"Wow. She left her fiancé at the altar?" He raised his brows at me. "Right off the bat, the two of you have something in common."

I sighed as I rolled my eyes.

"Did you at least get her phone number after you fucked her?"

"No, and stop saying it like that."

"Huh?" He looked at me in confusion. "Shit, Drew. What has this girl done to you?"

"I don't know." I turned my chair and looked out the window. "I put my number in her phone before I left. I told her if she ever needed anything to call me."

"Drew. Drew. Drew. Why didn't just tell her how much you liked her?"

"Because she's focusing on her journey and has made it very clear that she's living in a man-free zone."

"So what? You never let things stop you from going after what you want. Damn. Who are you and what have you done with Drew Westbrook?"

"Just drop it, Lance. Let's go. We have a meeting." I sighed as I got up from my seat.

Chapter Fourteen
Jillian

"It's so good to see you." Kristen hugged me tight as I stepped inside her apartment.

"It's good to see you too. How are you?" I broke our embrace.

"I'm okay. I just put on a fresh pot of coffee. You must be exhausted after that flight."

"Not really. I slept well on the plane."

My flight from Hawaii didn't get in to New York until ten a.m. I really had no choice but to sleep, because if I didn't, I would have spent the entire twelve hours thinking about Drew, and I was trying so hard to put him to rest. Following Kristen into the kitchen, I took a seat at the table while she poured us each a cup of coffee and set a plate of assorted donuts in the center of the table.

"My favorite." I smiled as I took a vanilla frosted one. "Did Noah go to work?"

"Yeah. He left about an hour ago. He said to tell you hello and that he'll see you later. So, tell me all about Hawaii."

As I sat across from Kristen, my heart felt sad seeing her so frail. Her skin was pale, her eyes were sunken in, and the beautiful blonde hair she once had was replaced by a headscarf. Six months ago, she was diagnosed with an inoperable brain tumor and had been undergoing chemotherapy and radiation to try and shrink it. Not only was she my best friend, she was also my half-sister. A sister I didn't even know I had until she contacted me, via Facebook, two years ago and asked if my father was Donald Bell. Our father had an affair with her mother when they met at a business conference. It lasted about a year until she told him she was pregnant. He gave her silence money to quietly walk away and agree to never let anyone know who the father was. He made her sign a contract that his crooked lawyer drew up stating that she wouldn't put him as the father on the birth certificate or ever disclose that he impregnated her. She saw what kind of man he was and took the money and ran as far away from him as she could. Before Kristen's mother passed away a couple of years ago, she told her everything about our dad. Who he was, where he lived, and about me.

When she contacted me, I wasn't surprised. I always suspected my father cheated on my mother. Kristen was my secret and I loved her; after all, we were sisters and only born one month apart. After she found me, we skyped almost every day and I came to New York a few times to visit her. Of course, I lied as to where I was going because if my parents ever found out that we found each other, it would open up a scandal that would rock the business world. It saddened me that my father could be so cold as to know he had another daughter and didn't care about how she grew up. He was a soulless man who was married to a soulless woman.

"Hawaii was great." I gave her a small smile.

"Did you by chance meet anyone there?" She grinned.

"You talked to Kellan. Didn't you?"

"Yeah." She took a sip from her cup.

"Drew is a great guy. He's fun, sweet, caring, and really hot."

"You slept with him, Jill. I can tell," she spoke with excitement.

"Ugh." I laid my head down on the table. "I didn't mean to. It just happened."

"And?"

Lifting my head, I looked up at her. "And then we said goodbye."

"You said that as if you were sad to say goodbye."

"Sort of. I don't know. Drew is —" I sighed. "He's the type of guy who I could see totally falling head over heels for."

Kristen gave me a small smile. "It looks to me like you already have."

"No." I held up my finger. "I'm in search of me, nobody else."

"Maybe you found yourself already the moment you sat next to him on the plane. The world works in mysterious ways, Jill. Of all the hotels in Hawaii, he stayed at the same one you did. Plus, he broke up with his girlfriend."

"I see Kellan filled you in on every little detail." I smiled. "I was going to tell you everything when I came here. I didn't want to burden you with my problems when you're going through so much already."

"But your problems are my problems, dear sister. Without your dysfunctional life, I'd be bored to death." She smiled.

I couldn't help but laugh. "You look tired." I pouted.

"I am. I hate that I feel like I need to go take a nap when you just got here."

"Go take a nap and when you wake up, we'll go to Central Park and sit under a big tree for some sisterly bonding time. In the meanwhile, I think I'll take a shower and change. I feel gross from the plane ride."

As the hot water streamed down my back, I couldn't stop thinking about Drew, and I wondered what he was doing and if he had heard from Jess. She didn't seem like the type of woman to go away quietly. Running my hands down my body, I swore I could still feel his tender touch. He was a god in the bedroom and I'd never had so many orgasms in such a short period of time in my life. I needed to put him to rest in the depths of my mind. I was living a single, free life now and nothing or no one was going to get in the way of that. My focus was solely on me now and, of course, my sister. She needed me. The only family she had left was Noah, her boyfriend of five years, and me.

Stepping out of the shower and wrapping a towel around me, I sat on the edge of the bed and dialed Kellan.

"Hello, Jilly Bean."

"Hey, Kel. I finally made it to New York."

"How's Kristen doing?"

"She's okay. She's napping right now and then I'm taking her to Central Park for a while. Any news on the home front?"

"I saw your mom yesterday and she gave me the evil eye." He laughed. "Then she had the nerve to come over and try to talk to me."

"What did she say?"

"Just asked if I heard from you yet and that she can't believe you would do what you did. She said poor Grant was so broken up, and that the wedding that didn't happen was the talk of the yacht club. She said she had to leave because of the embarrassment."

"Ha ha. Good."

"I told her that I saw Grant with some sleazy-looking chick the other night and he didn't look too broken up to me. She just huffed and said goodbye."

"Good for you. Thank you."

"Anything for you, babe. Hey, how about if I come to New York next weekend for a visit?"

"Ah. I would love that and so would Kristen and Noah."

"Are you going to get your own apartment there?"

"I was thinking about it, but I don't want to get stuck in a lease for a year. I may not be here that long."

"True. I'm sure you can find something with a six-month lease, or hell, just buy a place. It's not like you can't afford it. Then when you leave, rent it out, and it becomes an investment."

"I might just do that."

"Hey, how are you doing after your little romp with plane guy?"

"I'm okay."

"Jilly, that wasn't very convincing. Are you still thinking about him?"

"Sort of. He's a hard man to forget."

"Then maybe he's not worth forgetting. You have his number. Call him."

"I can't."

"You won't. I dig your whole self-journey, but if he put a real smile on that pretty face of yours, don't you think maybe, just maybe, he was thrown in your path for a reason?"

"Now you sound like Kristen."

"Great minds think alike. Listen, Bean, I have to go. I'm being summoned into a meeting. Love you."

"Love you. Talk to you soon."

I met Kellan Jones at the yacht club when were thirteen years old. His family had just moved to Seattle when his father took the CFO position for one of the biggest hotel chains in the country. It was love at first sight. We created a bond that day and had been best friends ever since. My parents disapproved at first because he was a boy and they feared some sort of romance was brewing. They couldn't grasp the concept that a boy and a girl could be nothing more than friends. There was a period of time when my parents tried to stop me from seeing Kellan, but that quickly dissipated when they found out he was gay and no longer a threat.

I wheeled Kristen to The Lake in Central Park. Since receiving her chemo and radiation treatments, she tired easily and walking would have been too much for her. I found us a spot on the grass under a big tree near the lake. After helping me spread out the blanket we brought, we both kicked off our shoes and sat down.

"God, it's so beautiful here," I spoke.

"It's one of my and Noah's favorite spots."

It was a beautiful June day. The sun was shining brightly and there wasn't a trace of wind anywhere. Despite all the people that were around, I found comfort and peace here.

"Tell me you have pictures of Hawaii." Kristin smiled.

"Of course I do," I spoke as I pulled my phone from my pocket.

Opening up my pictures, I began to show her the serenity and beautiful world of Hawaii.

"These are the dolphins I swam with." I smiled.

"Wow. They are adorable. I'd love to do that."

"You will. As soon as you get better, I'm taking you there and we'll swim with them."

She gave me a small, unconvincing smile. I knew exactly what that smile meant and it scared the hell out of me.

"Is this him?" she asked as she stopped on the picture of me and Drew.

My heart started to ache at the sight of him.

"Yes. That's Drew. I took that picture of us on our last night there."

"He's hot." She grinned.

The corners of my mouth curved slightly upwards. "Yeah. In more ways than one."

"Why did you take this picture?" she asked. "I mean, you knew you were never going to see him again and you have no plans of ever contacting him."

"I guess for a memory," I spoke in a mere whisper as I looked down at my hands.

"It's okay to like him, Jillian. You're human just like everyone else."

"If only I had met him a little later in life." I stared straight at the lake.

She reached over and took hold of my hand. "Sometimes life is too short to worry about the small stuff."

"You're going to be okay, Kristen. I truly believe that."

"Maybe or maybe not. And if not, I'm okay with that. I've come to terms that the chemo and radiation may not be helping."

I didn't like hearing her say that. It killed me inside to think that I might lose her. She had only been in my life for a short while and I wanted many more years with her. She was my sister and I needed her.

Chapter Fifteen
Drew

I had just returned from a meeting when I heard my office door open.

"You can't—" I heard Lia's voice.

"Oh please. And really? Those shoes?"

I turned around and clenched my jaw when I saw Jess.

"We need to talk, Drew." She stood there with her hand on her hip.

I sighed and took a seat behind my desk.

"Jess, what are you doing here? I told you that I didn't want to see you."

"I know, but I needed to see you. Please just hear me out."

"There's nothing to hear. It's over."

"Stop saying that. I'm sorry for everything. Please give me another chance. I can't bear to be without you." Tears started to stream down her face.

"No, Jess. It's over. You deserve someone who can give you everything you need." I got up from my chair, walked over to her, and clasped her shoulders. "I can't do that. And you know why I can't?"

She slowly shook her head.

"Because I'm not in love with you. I don't mean to hurt you, but it's how I feel and there's nothing you can do to change that."

Her bottom lip started to tremble. "But I need you. Don't you understand that?" Streaks of mascara ran down her face.

"You don't need me, Jess. You need a man who can love you back and I'm not that man."

"God, I hate you!" She began to pound her fists into my chest. "I spent a year with you. I gave you my everything. I gave you my heart and my love and this is how you repay me?"

I grabbed her wrists and held them tight so she'd stop pounding into me.

"Darling, the only thing you ever gave me was a headache. Now please leave before I call security."

Letting go of her wrists, I turned around and headed towards my desk.

"You'll regret this, Drew. You're going to wake up one day and realize what a mistake it was letting me go and then you'll be the one crawling back, begging me to take you back!" she shouted.

Rolling my eyes, I sighed. "Goodbye, Jess."

"Fuck you, Westbrook!" She stormed out of my office, slamming the door behind her.

After a few moments, when I knew she was out of sight, I opened the door, looked at Lia, and shrugged.

"She's crazy. What can I say?"

"You did the right thing, Drew. I didn't like her."

"Nobody did." I winked.

Lia, my secretary, was an excellent employee. She was a forty-year-old single mom of two girls. She came to work for me as a temp while my other secretary, Joy, was on maternity leave. When Joy decided to become a stay-at-home mom, I hired Lia right on the spot. She excelled at her work and needed the stability of a full-time permanent job so she could provide for her children since her deadbeat ex barely paid his child support.

"I need you to do me a favor," I spoke as I walked over to Lia's desk.

"Sure. Anything."

"See what you can find on a girl named Jillian Bell. She's from Seattle."

"Really?" The corners of her mouth curved upwards. "You've never done anything like that before."

"I know. I feel like a damn stalker."

"Who is she?"

"She's a woman that I spent some time with in Hawaii. Actually, we met on the plane. She had the seat next to mine and we stayed at the same hotel. Let's just say she's someone I can't get out of my head. Maybe you can track down a phone number or something."

"I'll see what I can do." She smiled.

"Thanks, Lia. I'll be in my office."

Just as I shut the door and was walking back to my desk, my phone rang and it was my mom.

"Hey, Mom."

"Drew. How was Hawaii?"

"It was good." *Only good because of Jillian.*

"Did you and Jess get some things worked out?"

I leaned back in my chair. "We sure did. I ended things with her."

"Oh?" There was a hint of excitement in her voice.

"It's okay, Mom. Just say it."

"You want the truth, Drew?"

"Of course I do."

"I'm happy you ended it with that little witch. You know how your father and I felt about her."

"I know you didn't like her and I'm sorry I didn't end things sooner."

"Well, what matters is that you did end it. Listen, honey, I have to get going. Why don't you come over tomorrow night for a barbeque?"

"Sounds good, Mom. I'll be there."

After ending the call, I set my phone down on my desk. I wished they could have met Jillian. She was the type of girl that my mom would fall in love with.

"Excuse me, Drew," Lia softly spoke as she poked her head in the door.

"Come on in. Did you find anything?"

"The only thing I could find on Jillian Bell was this article." She handed me a white sheet of paper. "I don't think that's her, right?"

"That's her." I smiled as I stared at her picture.

"She left her fiancé on their wedding day?" she asked with a twisted face.

"Yep, and for good reason. Her story is a little complicated."

"She's pretty."

"Pretty is an understatement. She's a beautiful woman with a beautiful soul."

"I'm sorry that's all I could find, Drew."

"It's okay, Lia. Thank you."

I could have just hired a private investigator to find her, but I wouldn't do that. I said goodbye to her for a reason and I wasn't going to interfere with her life. As badly as I missed her and wanted to talk to her, I needed to respect her journey. I had no clue what I was thinking when I asked Lia to see what she could find out. Jillian had my number and, hopefully, one day, she'd think of me and call.

****

Jillian

When Kristen and I walked through the doors of The Ellington on West 52nd Street, we stepped inside the elevator and took it up to the 28th floor where I was meeting, Rick, the realtor who was going to show me the apartment.

"Hello, you must be Jillian." Rick smiled as he held out his hand.

"Nice to meet you, Rick."

"My pleasure, and this is?" he asked as he looked at Kristen.

"I'm the sister." She smiled.

"Ah. Nice to meet you. If you'll follow me, I'll show you around this gorgeous apartment. Will it just be you living here, Jillian?"

"Yes." I smiled as I looked around.

"Then this is the place for you. Come over here," he spoke as he led me to the balcony off the living room. "Look at this view. You can practically see the entire city from up here, and at night, it's gorgeous. All you need are a couple of lounge chairs, a small table, and an expensive bottle of wine." He winked.

"What do you think, Kristen?" I asked.

"I think this place is great. I could totally see you making this space your very own."

"Me too." I smiled as I continued to look around.

"Oh, and the best part is that the laundry room is right down the hall."

"That's a plus. How much is the rent again?" I asked.

"Forty-five hundred."

"Okay. I'll take it."

"Excellent." Rick clapped his hands together. "I will let the owner know and I'll draw up the lease agreement. How soon do you want to move in?"

"This weekend if possible."

"Perfect. I will call you in a couple of days when the paperwork is ready, you can swing by the office to sign them, and I'll hand you the keys."

"Great. I look forward to it."

****

Drew

I had just arrived home from work when my phone rang.

"Hey, Rick," I answered.

"Drew, I have great news. I rented your apartment today to a very nice young woman. She'll be moving in this weekend."

"Ah. Excellent news. Thanks for letting me know."

"Any time, buddy. Have a good night."

"You too."

Chapter Sixteen
Jillian

In my hand, I held the keys to my very own apartment. I'd never had my own place before. Even when I was in college, I lived with Grant.

"How about we do a little furniture shopping?" I smiled at Kristen.

"Sounds like fun. I love to shop for furniture."

I hooked my arm in hers as we exited the realtor's office and headed to the nearest furniture store.

"Hello." A nice-looking young man smiled at us as we walked through the door.

"Hi."

"Can I help you?"

"Actually, I'm going to be spending a lot of money in this store today to furnish my new apartment."

"Excellent." He grinned as he saw dollar signs and a nice commission check. "I'm Heath." He politely stuck out his hand.

"I'm Jillian and this is my sister, Kristen."

"Nice to meet you ladies. Where shall we start?"

Looking at my watch, I spoke, "It's two o'clock. How about we start with a glass of wine? You do have wine, right?" I smiled.

"Of course. Red or white?"

"White will be fine. We're going to look around."

"Please do. I'll go fetch some wine and I'll come find you."

"Thank you, Heath."

He gave me a smile as he walked away. He was cute with his six-foot stature, short blonde spikey hair, and green eyes.

"So where do you want to start?" Kristen asked.

"Let's start with the living room first," I spoke as I headed over to some displays.

Heath walked over and handed each of us a glass of wine. "See anything that catches your eye?" he asked.

"Actually," I smiled, "I think I may like that couch over there." I pointed.

Walking over to where the dark gray leather reclining couch sat, I took a seat and instantly fell in love.

"Nice color," Kristen spoke as she sat down next to me.

"Isn't it? Patricia hates gray." I smirked. "She says it's the worst color in the world and is a reflection of the person who chooses to decorate in such a drab, boring color."

"Then it's the perfect color for your apartment." She grabbed hold of my hand.

"May I make a suggestion?" Heath asked.

"Of course, Heath. Suggest away." I smiled as I took a sip from my glass.

"Follow me."

Kristen and I got up from the couch and followed him over to a display where a dark red chaise lounge sat.

"Oh. I love this," I said as I ran my hand along the fabric.

"Isn't it fabulous? Envision it next to the gray couch you were looking at. And right over here, we have this lovely red square cocktail ottoman you can use as a coffee table."

"Perfect. Sold, Heath." I grinned. "Now I need a TV. I'll be hanging it on the wall."

"Our TV selection is over this way." He waved.

After picking out my living room furniture, dining table, and some lamps, Kristen and I headed over to the bedroom sets. There was one bed that caught my attention very quickly. It was an upholstered sleigh bed in a color called gunmetal. While Kristen was with Heath looking at another bedroom set, I made myself comfortable across the bed.

"Excellent choice," Heath spoke as he walked over. "This is our new Bombay collection that just arrived a few days ago."

Kristen lay down next to me and we both stared up at the ceiling.

"This would be the perfect bed to fuck in." She smiled as she looked over at me.

Suddenly, visions of my and Drew's night together filled my mind.

"It would be. Too bad it won't be getting any kind of action."

"Maybe not with two people, but maybe with one." She laughed.

"True. Very true, dear sister."

Heath cleared his throat to alert us he could hear our conversation. Getting up from the bed, I placed my hand on his chest.

"Don't feel sorry for me, Heath. It's my own choice."

As I was paying for my new furniture, my phone rang. It was Kellan.

"Hey, I can't wait to show you my new apartment."

"I can't come to New York this weekend, Jilly."

"Why?" I whined.

"My mom is having surgery tomorrow and my dad is on a business trip over in London."

"Is she okay?"

"She's having her breast implants taken out. Both of them are leaking and they need to come out as soon as possible. So I have to take care of her until my dad can get back home."

"Okay. Give your mom a huge hug and kiss from me and I hope she recovers quickly. Maybe you can come the following weekend."

"I'm already planning on it. Love you, Bean."

"Love you too, Kel. Talk to you later."

The Exception

****

Moving into my new apartment was the easiest job ever. The deliverymen set up all my furniture and it didn't take me long to unpack the only two suitcases I brought with me. Looking around my space made me smile. This was mine. My very own apartment and a symbol of a new start in life for me. I felt independent and I felt strong. Two things that I had never felt before.

Three years ago, on my twenty-first birthday, I received a call from my grandmother's lawyer, asking me to come to his office. I found it strange since my grandmother had passed away two years before. When I arrived at his office, he informed me that my grandmother had set up an account for me with the sum of four million dollars to be given to me on my twenty-first birthday with a letter she had written to me.

My dearest Jillian,

Happy birthday, my darling granddaughter. Now that you are coming into the age of adulthood, I am giving you something special for those rainy days. This is between me and you and your parents are never to know what I have given you. Use the money to do what you want in life. It's yours and yours only. Travel. See the world and, whatever you do, do not marry Grant. I don't like him, darling. I never have and, most importantly, do not trust him. He doesn't make you happy and you deserve to be happy. I know you'll make the right decision one day and this money will be there to help you. Take care, my love. I'll love you forever.

Grandma

My grandmother and I were very close and I told her everything. She was never very fond of my mother and she'd tell my father every chance she got. She hadn't spoken to my parents for a few years before she passed. I still didn't know what the argument was about, but I suspected it had something to do with Kristen. I'd never forget after she passed away and we were all gathered at the table for the reading of the will. When it came to my father and mother, they were given nothing. My grandmother left her whole estate to my Uncle Leon with the strict instructions that all of her clothes and jewelry were to be donated to a women's shelter and my mother was not to be given anything. My parents were outraged and my mom didn't stop yelling for months over it. As for me, she had left me ten thousand dollars and a beautiful silver necklace with a diamond cross that I'd always admired.

After Kristen and Noah left, I grabbed the open bottle of wine from the counter and took it outside on the balcony where I sat my ass down in my new plush and comfortable lounge chair. Rick was right; sitting out here at night looking at the brightly lit city was amazing. I hadn't thought about Drew all day until now. As I held my phone in my hand, I pulled up his number and stared at it. A part of me wanted to get in touch with him just to say hi. But the other part of me didn't want to because I knew if I did, I would never stop thinking about him or that night we spent together. I just wanted to hear his voice. Maybe if I just heard it one last time, thoughts of him would leave my head. This was crazy. This wasn't me. I didn't think like this and I certainly didn't just call up people to hear their voice. What the fuck was going on? Why for the love of God couldn't I get him out of my head? I set my number to private and hit the call button under his number. My heart started pounding out of my chest. It was Saturday night so he probably wouldn't answer. I would bet he was out with someone for the night. The hand that held the phone to my ear started to sweat.

"Drew Westbrook," he answered.

SHIT!

"Hello?"

If I didn't say something, he'd probably suspect it was me, so I cleared my throat and disguised my voice.

"I'm sorry. I have the wrong number."

"No problem," he spoke.

I quickly ended the call. Wow, what did I just do? Who does that? A small smile crossed my lips as I set my phone down. Hearing his voice again was exactly what I needed. I could hear a lot of noise in the background, almost as if he was at a restaurant. The thought of him with another woman literally knifed my heart. *Fuck!* I didn't need this. This wasn't how my life journey was supposed to go. I wasn't supposed to be thinking about a man. I certainly had no problem forgetting about one in particular. Damn Drew Westbrook. I finished off the bottle of wine and climbed into my new comfy bed.

Chapter Seventeen
Drew

"Who was that?" Liam asked as he raised his brow at me.

"Just a wrong number." I frowned as I looked at my phone and set it on the table. "It's weird because it came up as a private number."

Liam shrugged. "People do that all the time. No big deal."

"Yeah, I guess." I took a drink of my scotch.

"I'm sorry your Hawaii trip sucked."

"It only sucked when Jess was around." I cut into my steak.

"Yeah, well, she was a sucky person." He smiled. "Now you're back on the market. Any prospects yet?"

"Actually, I met a woman in Hawaii."

"Damn, you work fast." He winked.

"She sat next to me on the plane from Seattle to LAX, we had dinner at the airport together, and then I switched seats so I could sit next to her to Hawaii. Coincidentally, she ended up staying at the same hotel."

Liam narrowed his eye at me. "You slept with her, didn't you?"

"Yep. On my last night there after I broke up with Jess. It wasn't planned. It just happened. I really like her a lot."

"Okay. So where's she from? Did you get her number?"

"Life is a little complicated for her right now."

"How so?"

"She comes from a very controlling family and she left her fiancé at the altar on their wedding day to go on a journey of self-discovery. So I have no clue where she went when she left Hawaii."

The waitress walked over and cleared our plates from the table.

"Can I get you anything else?"

"Another round of scotch for me and my friend."

"Coming right up." She winked at me.

"I think someone likes you." Liam smirked.

I rolled my eyes. "I can't even explain the connection I felt with Jillian. I don't know, man. I've never felt like this before towards someone. It's really bothering me."

"Sounds to me like you're in love. Maybe for the first real time in your life." He smiled.

"I don't know. But what I do know is that I want to see her again. I gave her my number before I left in case she ever needed anything."

"Maybe that was her who called."

"Nah. It didn't sound like her at all. She's never going to call and I just need to accept that. She's doing her own thing and finding herself. I'm sure she hasn't even given me another thought."

"I'm sorry, man, but chin up. There's plenty of other women in the world who would love to go out with you."

"What if I would have said that to you about Avery?" I picked up my drink.

His narrowed eye continued to stare at me for a moment. "It's that serious?"

"It is."

****

Jillian

I awoke to my ringing phone, and when I looked at the clock, it was six thirty a.m.

"Noah, what's wrong?" I asked.

"I brought Kristen to the ER a couple of hours ago. She had a fever of 104.9 and she was hallucinating."

"I'm on my way. Which hospital are you at?"

"Mount Sinai. Text me when you get here and I'll find you. I think they're getting ready to take her up to a room."

"Okay."

I quickly jumped out of bed, threw on some clothes, and ran a brush through my hair. Grabbing my purse, I flew out the door and hailed a cab.

"Mount Sinai," I told the cab driver as I climbed inside.

A nervous feeling ran deep inside me. I was scared for my sister and my nerves were getting the best of me.

"Can you please step on it!" I yelled.

"Lady, this is New York traffic. What do you want me to do?"

"I'm sorry. I just need to get to my sister."

Finally, we made it to the hospital and the cab driver dropped me off in front of the ER. I handed him some money, and when I walked through the doors, I sent Noah a text message. After pacing around the lobby for what seemed like forever, the elevator doors opened and Noah stepped out.

"How is she?"

"She's resting and they have her on some strong antibiotics. The doctor said she has a bacterial infection and he's calling her oncologist."

"She was fine yesterday," I spoke.

"I know. It was shortly after we got home from your place that she said she was really tired and not feeling well."

Hooking my arm around him, we took the elevator up to the third floor where her room was. When I walked in, she slowly opened her eyes and a small smile crossed her lips.

"How are you feeling?" I asked as I walked over and took hold of her hand.

"Like shit. But I'm glad you're here."

"There's nowhere else I'd be." I gently gave her hand a squeeze.

After talking with her for a few minutes, she started to close her eyes.

"You get some rest. I'm going to grab a coffee. Noah, why don't you go home and get some sleep. You look tired and I'm here. She's probably going to be out for a while."

"I don't want to leave her, Jill."

"Then sleep in the chair for a bit. Okay?"

"Yeah. Maybe I will. Thanks."

Walking down the hallway, I found a waiting room with a coffee machine. After inserting some money, I pushed the button and waited patiently for the cup to drop.

"Really?" I said out loud as no cup appeared.

I wasn't in the mood for this shit, so I banged the machine.

"Consider yourself lucky. That machine has the worst coffee," a nurse spoke as she walked up next to me. "You can grab some in the cafeteria. In fact, I'm heading down there now and I can show you the way."

"Thank you. I'm sorry for banging on the machine."

"Please, honey. Don't apologize. Those machines deserve to be beat on every once in a while. I'm Andrea. I saw you and Noah walking into Kristen's room. Are you a friend?"

"I'm Jillian and I'm her sister."

"Nice to meet you, Jillian. Your sister is a wonderful girl."

"You know her?" I asked as we stepped into the cafeteria.

"I'm usually her nurse when she comes in for her chemo treatments. Today was supposed to be my day off, but they had quite a few call ins and asked if I could help out. I never turn down overtime." She smiled. "I've never seen you here with your sister. Are you from out of town?" she asked as she grabbed a bagel.

I was starving and they did look good, so I grabbed one as well.

"I lived in Seattle and I just moved to New York last week."

"Welcome to New York." She smiled. "Would you like to join me?"

"Sure." I paid for my coffee and bagel and the two of us took a seat at a small table by the window.

There was something about Andrea that made me feel very comfortable. I couldn't exactly put my finger on it, but she was one of those people that you could just instantly connect with.

"Did you move here with someone?" she asked.

"No. I moved here alone. My life is a little complicated at the moment."

Why did I just tell her that?

"Isn't everyone's life a little complicated from time to time?" she smiled.

"Yeah. Maybe."

After talking for a while and finishing our bagel and coffee, we headed back up to the third floor. When I walked into Kristen's room, she was awake.

"Hey, you. Where were you?"

"I was in the cafeteria having breakfast with your nurse, Andrea."

"I'm glad you met her. I knew you'd like her."

Just as Noah woke up, Kristen's doctor walked in.

"So, missy. It looks like you have a bacterial infection, eh?"

"That's what they tell me, Dr. Jenkins."

"Your immune system is down from the chemo and radiation. I know you have an appointment on Monday for another scan, but since you're here, we might as well do it now. Are you okay with that?"

"Do I have a choice?" Kristen smirked.

"No. Not really. I'll go order it and someone will be here soon to take you down."

"Thanks."

"You're welcome. I'll talk to you later."

After he walked out of the room, Andrea walked in with a warm blanket and draped it over Kristen.

"There you go, honey. We need to keep you nice and warm."

"Thanks, Andrea. By the way, how's your son and girlfriend doing?"

"Oh, good news. He finally dumped her. Hearing him say that was music to my ears." She winked before leaving the room.

"Sounds like everyone is getting dumped these days." I laughed.

"She couldn't stand that woman. On my chemo days, she'd tell me how much of a bitch she was and that her son could do so much better. She couldn't understand what he saw in her besides her big fake tits." She laughed. "Her words, not mine."

It wasn't too long before the transporter walked into the room and took Kristen for her scan. Noah went with her and I stayed back in the room and waited for them. Pulling out my phone, I decided to give Kellan a call to tell him about Kristen and to ask how his mom was doing. But before I could dial him, like an idiot, I opened up my photos and stared at the selfie Drew and I took after we swam with the dolphins. My heart started to ache and I hated the sadness that overtook me every time I looked at that damn picture.

"You okay, honey?" Andrea asked as she walked into the room.

Closing out of the picture, I looked up at her, and instead of saying a simple yes, words just came falling out of my mouth.

"I don't know. I met this guy when I was on a trip and I can't stop thinking about him. It's like he's in my head twenty-four hours a day."

"Where's he from?"

"I don't know. I didn't ask and I didn't want to know because I'm not in the dating zone, so to speak. I'm rediscovering myself and there's no room in my life for a man right now."

"May I ask why you're rediscovering yourself?"

"Long story. My parents are very rich and influential. They molded me into someone I'm not nor do I want to be. I ran away." I looked down. "And I'm never going back."

"Kristen never mentioned that about her parents."

"That's because Kristen and I only share the same father. A father who paid her mother off never to tell anyone who her father is. He's never acknowledged her and he's never met her."

"Oh."

"I've only known that I had a sister for a couple of years and that's only because she found me."

Andrea walked over and sat on the edge of the bed next to me.

"What have you found out so far about yourself?" she asked as she placed her hand on mine.

"That I love being on my own but also that I have this need to feel safe. The guy I was talking about earlier made me feel that way. Even though I'd only known him for a few days, it felt like I'd known him for years. He made me feel secure, even though I had always thought I felt it. But apparently, I didn't."

"Sounds like you're in love with this man." She smiled.

"How could I be? I barely know him."

"Doesn't matter, honey. You don't have to know him to feel it. It's instant chemistry, divine intervention, soul mates. Whatever you want to call it, it's just there. My thought on the whole thing is if you're meant to be together, you will be. Maybe not now, or next year, but some time in this life." She winked. "I have to go check on my patients. I'll talk to you later."

"Thanks, Andrea."

"You're welcome, sweetheart."

I stayed with Kristen the rest of the day until she kicked me out and ordered me to go home.

"I'll be back tomorrow." I kissed her forehead.

"Looking forward to it." She smiled.

Chapter Eighteen
Jillian

The next day, as I was arranging the bouquet of flowers I picked up for Kristen, Dr. Jenkins walked in. I swallowed hard when I saw the look on his face.

"I have the results of your scan, Kristen," he softly spoke.

Noah and I both grabbed hold of her hands while we waited for the doctor to give her the results.

"How long do I have?" she bravely asked.

"Anywhere from six to nine months. But nine months is stretching it. The cancer has spread to other areas of the brain."

It felt like the air had been knocked out of me and to breathe was nearly impossible. Tears started to stream down Noah's face, and as I looked at Kristen, she remained composed and calm, as if she already knew what he was going to say.

"Thank you, Dr. Jenkins," she spoke. "I know you've done everything you could."

"Again, I'm sorry. You're far too young to have to go through this. You can go home tomorrow, but you'll still need to be on antibiotics for the bacterial infection," he spoke before walking out of the room.

Tears started to pour from my eyes. I knew I needed to be strong for her, but I couldn't be. This was too much of a shock. Noah buried his head into her arm and sobbed. The only one in the room who wasn't crying was Kristen and I couldn't understand why. Maybe it hadn't hit her yet.

"I'm so sorry." I bawled like a baby.

"The two of you have about five minutes left of crying time and then it stops. I was prepared for this. I knew deep down that I wasn't going to get better. I made peace with it already and I need you both to do the same. I'm not afraid to die."

After drying my eyes, I stepped out of the room to give her and Noah time alone. Walking out of the hospital, I put on my sunglasses and took a seat on a bench underneath a large tree. The tears wouldn't stop falling and I had never felt so alone. She was my sister, she was dying, and I had no one to talk to, right here, right now. I tried to call Kellan and he didn't answer, so I pulled up Drew's number. He said if I ever needed anything to call him. But what did I actually need? To hear his voice? Maybe. No. I wasn't going to burden him with my problems. I had never even mentioned Kristen to him. Anyway, I was sure he'd already forgotten about me and the fact that he even gave me his number. I needed to grow the hell up and push my feelings about this aside for now and be there for my sister. I couldn't let her see me crumble into a million pieces.

As I approached her room, I stood in the doorway and stared at her.

"Where have you been?" she softly spoke.

"Outside, sitting on a bench under a large tree." I gently grinned.

"Okay. I get it. You needed your time to absorb what Dr. Jenkins said."

"Where's Noah?" I asked as I sat down on the edge of her bed.

"He's calling his family." She grabbed my hand. "Listen, I'm going to make the most of the time I have left and that doesn't include watching the people I love being upset. Jill, you have to understand that I was prepared for this, so it's not news to me."

"How the fuck are you so strong?" I pouted.

"I get it from my mom. She wasn't afraid to die and neither am I. I know it's hard on you and Noah. If the situation was reversed, I'd be devastated, but I need you to just go on. Live your life as if I wasn't dying. I intend to and I'm going to make each day worth it. Would you like to take a painting class with me?" She smiled.

"A painting class?" I cocked my head.

"Yes. I've always wanted to take one and, damn it, I'm going to do it before it's too late."

"I'd love to take a painting class with you. Would you like me to set it up?"

"Nope. I'll do it and I'll let you know when it is."

I leaned over and hugged her. "You are so brave, my dear sister."

"It runs in our family." She smiled. "You're the brave one for leaving your family behind and starting a new life. Not many people can do that."

"I didn't leave my family behind. You're my family and all the family I need."

Noah walked back into the room with his parents and, immediately, his mother started to cry.

"Go home now. There's no reason for you to stay and witness this. I'm fine and I'll call you later."

"Are you sure?" I asked.

"Very sure." She gave a small smile. "You better go fix your eyes. They're a mess."

"I know." I put my sunglasses back on.

I gave her a kiss and hugged Noah goodbye. As I stepped out of the hospital, the once bright blue sunny sky had turned gray and now it was raining. I wasn't ready to go home yet. Walking back into the hospital, I stopped at the gift shop and picked up an umbrella. I decided to leave my sunglasses on to hide the fact that I'd been crying. If I was going to walk around the streets of New York City, I didn't need people staring at me.

Walking down Madison Ave, I stared straight ahead as I held the umbrella over my head. My shoes sloshed on the wet pavement as the rain poured down. Kristen told me not to be sad, but how could I not be? She was the only person I had left in this world and now she was being taken away from me. The rain suddenly stopped and the sun appeared from amongst the clouds. As I was closing my umbrella, I pulled my ringing phone from my pocket. When I looked down at it, I saw Kellan was calling.

"Oh, excuse me," a man's voice spoke and his hand lightly touched my arm as he walked by.

"I'm sor—" I turned around and gasped. "Drew?" I shouted.

He stopped dead in his tracks and stood there for a second before turning around.

"Jillian?"

"Yes!" My heart started pounding.

He walked towards me and stopped as he stood there and stared at me.

"What—I can't believe—oh my God." He wrapped his arms around me.

"What are you doing here?" I asked.

"I live here. What are you doing here?" He broke our embrace and stared at me through my sunglasses.

"I live here too. This is where I came right from Hawaii."

His lips curved up into a small smile while he removed my sunglasses from my face. Our eyes locked onto each other and his smile drifted away.

"You've been crying," he spoke as he took his thumbs and tried to wipe away the stains under my eyes. "What happened?"

"Long story." I looked down.

"I've got all the time in the world. Do you want to grab a bite to eat? Or we can go somewhere and talk."

"I am starving. I haven't eaten all day."

"Then let's go get something to eat." He smiled as he held his arm out and I hooked mine around his. "There's Serafina's right across the street if you like pizza or pasta."

"That's fine. I really need a drink."

Per Drew's request, we were seated in a round corner booth away from the crowd that occupied the restaurant.

"Hello, my name is Kim and I'll be taking your order. May I start you off with something to drink?"

"I'll have a glass of Moscato, please," I replied.

"Just bring the whole bottle and two glasses," Drew told her.

He reached across the table and took hold of my hand, gently rubbing his thumb across my skin. Feeling his warm touch soothed me and I still couldn't believe he was here."

"I can't believe I'm sitting across from you right now." He smiled. "I thought I'd never see you again."

"I know, right? I can't believe it either."

"Tell me what's wrong, Jillian. Why were you crying?"

I swallowed hard and then took in a deep breath.

"It's my sister, Kristen."

"I thought you were an only child?"

"Remember when you asked if I was an only child and I said sort of but that's another story?"

"Yes. I remember."

"I have a half-sister and her name is Kristen. She was the product of an affair that my father had years ago. She found me and we connected. About six months ago, she was diagnosed with an inoperable brain tumor. She went through chemo and radiation with the hopes that the tumor had shrunk. But it didn't and she was told today that the cancer spread and she has about six to nine months left to live." My eyes started to water.

The waitress set down two glasses and poured some wine into each of them.

"Excuse me, where's your restrooms?" I asked.

"Right behind you, sweetie." She gave me a sad and pathetic look.

"Hold your thoughts." I looked at Drew. "I'm going to clean myself up a bit."

"Okay. Take as much time as you need."

Chapter Nineteen
Drew

I couldn't believe she was here in New York. Seeing her again was a dream come true. Man, the news about her sister tore at my heart. Pulling out my phone, I called Lia.

"Mr. Westbrook's office."

"Lia, it's me. I'm not coming back to the office today. Clear my schedule."

"Is everything okay, Drew?" she asked.

"Everything's fine. I'll talk to you tomorrow."

Just as I ended the call, Jillian walked back to the table.

"Better?" she asked.

"I didn't think you looked bad to begin with." I smiled.

She sat down and I immediately reached for her hand.

"I'm sorry about your sister. I can only imagine what you're going through right now."

"Thank you. I just can't absorb it."

"How is she doing?"

I let out a light laugh. "She was prepared for this and already accepted it. She's acting like it's no big deal and that's what I can't understand. And poor Noah."

"Her husband?" I asked.

"Her boyfriend. He just sobbed like I'd never seen a man sob before. It's weird, Drew. She's so strong, she doesn't seem scared, and she said she's not afraid to die."

"Maybe she isn't and you need to believe her. Whether you think it's weird or not, you have to respect what she says and how she feels."

"I know and I do. Anyway, enough about me. I can't believe you live in New York."

"I can't believe you moved to New York." I smirked.

"I'm afraid to ask," she spoke as she picked up her glass of wine. "Have you heard from Jess?"

I sighed. "Oh yeah. She came storming into my office the other day begging me to take her back."

"Did you?"

"Of course not. I told her that she deserved someone who could love her because I didn't. The thing is everyone is happy I broke up with her. She wasn't very popular with my friends and family."

"I can understand why." She laughed.

"It's good to see you laugh, Jillian."

She held up her glass to me. "Thank you again, Mr. Westbrook, for making my shitty day a little less shitty."

"It's my pleasure." I winked. We talked a little more while we ate and then I called Roland to bring the car around.

"Let me drive you home."

"I can catch a cab. I don't want you going out of your way."

"It's not out of my way and I want to."

Roland pulled up and I opened the door for her.

"It's not an option. I'm taking you home."

"Well, if you insist." She smiled.

Fuck. I couldn't even begin to explain the feelings that soared through me. I was happy and I didn't want to say goodbye. All I wanted to do was tell her that I really liked her and that I wanted to spend as much time with her as possible. But I couldn't. I didn't want to cause any waves or rock the boat, so to speak.

"Where to?" I asked.

"The Ellington on West 52nd Street, please."

"Seriously?"

"Yeah. Why?"

"No reason. That's a really nice building. They have some great apartments."

"I know. I just moved in a few days ago and I absolutely love it."

There was no way. No way at all she was the one who rented my apartment. It was just a coincidence. When Roland pulled up to the building, I opened the door, climbed out, and held out my hand to her.

"Would you like to come up and see my apartment?" she asked.

Perfect. I was hoping she'd ask so I didn't have to.

"I'd love to."

As we stepped into the elevator, she pushed the button to the twenty-eighth floor. It was her. The woman of my dreams was the one who rented my apartment.

"Well, here it is." She smiled as she opened the door.

"Nice furniture. I like the color scheme."

"Thanks. My mom hates those colors." She grinned.

I walked around the space that I once called home. Telling her that I was her landlord was going to be fun.

"I like the way you placed your furniture. If it was my place, I would have put my couch this way and the chairs over here. But the way you did it looks great too."

I walked into the bedroom. "My bed would have been placed here. Not where you have it, but it looks good there." I winked as she stood there, narrowing her eyes at me. Walking out of the bedroom and over to the balcony door, I opened it. "Make sure that you have the lock on the knob unlocked before stepping onto the balcony. It's one of those that doesn't feel like it's locked from the inside, but if you turn the knob from the outside, it's locked. See." I smiled. "You wouldn't want to get locked out there. It's not fun."

"How did you know that?" She shook her head in confusion.

With a grin, I held out my hand. "It's nice to meet you, Miss Bell. I'm Drew Westbrook, your landlord."

"Huh?" Her eyes widened.

"No handshake for your landlord?"

She gently placed her hand in mine. "Wait a minute! This is your apartment?!"

I chuckled. "Yes. This is my apartment."

"And you used to live here?"

"Yes, before I bought my townhouse. I kept it for an investment."

She placed her hands on her head. "This is literally fucking crazy, Drew."

"I know." I laughed.

"So you knew I was here in New York?"

"No. Everything is handled through my realtor. Rick just called and told me that a nice young woman rented it. I had no clue it was you."

Placing my hands on her hips, I spoke, "Weird, right?"

"I have no words right now. This is totally crazy." She smiled.

All I wanted to do was feel the softness of her lips again. As I stared into her blue eyes, she stared back at me. Should I risk it? Maybe she didn't want me to kiss her? But I'd never know until I tried and I wasn't about to let this opportunity escape me. Brushing a strand of hair from her face, I tucked it behind her ear and leaned in, brushing my lips against hers. She returned my kiss and placed her hands on my chest. Our tongues softly tangled as our lips gently touched. Nothing hot and heavy yet. I needed to respect her boundaries.

"I couldn't stop thinking about you since I left Hawaii," I quietly spoke in between kisses.

"I couldn't either."

I broke our kiss. "You couldn't stop thinking about you either?" I smirked.

Her hand lightly smacked my chest.

"No. I thought about you all the time."

"Then why didn't you call?"

She sighed and turned her back to me. "I did."

A smile crossed my lips. "The other night? That was you?"

"Yeah. Sorry about that. I just—" She paused.

"Just what, Jillian?"

"I just wanted to hear a familiar voice."

Wrapping my arms around her from behind, I kissed the side of her neck.

"I'm happy you did. But I do have a question."

"What?" She turned around in my arms.

"You could have easily known that I was from New York just by the area code."

"Oh. To be honest, I didn't even pay attention."

"Do you want me to leave?" I asked as I ran my thumb across her lips.

"It's probably for the best. Right now isn't a good time."

"You're right. I'm happy you're here." I smiled as I kissed her forehead. "Give me a call, okay? And don't have your number on private."

"I will and I won't."

Chapter Twenty
Jillian

Drew gave me one more kiss before I walked him to the door.

"Bye, Jillian." He smiled as he ran his hand across my cheek.

"Bye, Drew."

He walked out and I shut the door. I had thought about that man since the day I met him and I just let him walk out. Oh hell no. What was I thinking? Fuck my journey for right now. I wanted sex with him again. I needed sex with him. I opened the door and stepped out into the hallway.

"Drew!" I shouted as he was about to step onto the elevator.

"Something wrong?" He turned and looked at me.

"Yeah. I don't want you to go." I smiled. "See, I have this brand new bed that needs to be broken in."

Suddenly, the door across from me opened and an elderly woman stood there staring at me.

"Hi, Mrs. Lowe." Drew waved as he walked towards me.

"Hello, Drew. Nice to see you again. What's going on out here?"

"Nothing. Just dropped by to meet my new tenant."

"Hmm." She looked me up and down, gave me a wink, and then shut her door.

"Oops." I laughed as I placed my hand over my mouth.

"Now take me to this new bed of yours." Drew smiled as he placed his arm around me.

"Since you lived here, why don't you lead the way?"

Drew picked me up, kissed my lips, and then took me to the bedroom. Gently laying me down on the bed, he hovered over me as his lips pressed tightly against mine. His erection pressed firmly against me, making my desire for him even stronger. I tilted my head back so his tongue could stroke my neck. Even though I'd only felt it one time before, it was incredible enough for me to remember. Soft moans escaped me as his hand crept up my shirt and brushed against the fabric of my bra, pulling the cup down and running his fingers along my hardened nipple.

"I couldn't stop thinking about our night together," he whispered.

"Me either," I spoke breathlessly.

He climbed off of me and unbuttoned his shirt. Sliding it off his shoulders, I gasped at the sight of his ripped body, something I had longed to see again. Sitting up, I lifted my shirt over my head and tossed it to the side and then took down my pants as Drew took down his.

"Leave your panties on." He smiled. "I want to take them off myself."

I swallowed hard as I could feel the wetness pour from me already. He leaned over and his hands reached behind and unhooked my bra. Slowly taking one strap down at a time, he kissed my shoulders before removing my bra completely and throwing it on the floor.

"You are drop dead gorgeous," he spoke as his mouth explored each breast.

Pushing me down on my back, he hovered over me once again and his hand found its way to my wet spot as his fingers gently played with me and his lips were on mine. Excitement tore through me like a fierce storm.

"Fuck, you're so wet." He broke our kiss. "I want to taste you again." His eyes bore into mine.

"I want you to," I spoke with bated breath.

His hands took hold of my waist as I arched my back in anticipation for what he was about to do to me. The light stroke of his tongue against my clit set my body on fire and it wasn't too long before an earth-shattering orgasm fell upon me.

"Oh my God!" I yelped as my hands tangled through his hair while his face was between my legs.

Once I came down from my orgasm, his tongue slid up my slick spot, to my abdomen and over each breast while his fingers dipped inside me. He had just sent me to the moon and back and everything that I was going through in my life suddenly disappeared.

"I need to be inside you, babe. Are you still on birth control?"

"Yes. But wait."

I thought it was only right to repay the favor. I began to sit up and he rolled off of me.

"What's wrong?"

"Nothing." I smiled. "Sit up." I lightly wrapped my fingers around his hard, throbbing cock.

The smile on his face grew wide as I scooted off the bed and got down on my knees. He inched his body closer to the edge as my lips wrapped themselves around his manhood.

"Jesus, Jillian. Oh my God. That feels so incredible."

His hands placed themselves on my head as I continued to explore him with my mouth.

"As much as I love this, you need to stop or I'm going to come. Get up here," he commanded.

Removing my mouth and slowly licking my lips, I climbed on top of him and smiled.

"I hope you enjoyed that."

"You have no idea." He grabbed the back of my head and brought me down to his lips.

Rolling me over, he hovered over me as he quickly thrust inside me. Gasping as his entire length devoured me, I wrapped my legs around his waist as his thrusts became faster and deeper.

"Is this how you like it?" he asked breathlessly.

"Yes. Oh yes." My body prepared for another orgasm.

"You're going to come with me. I'm going to hold back as long as I can until you're ready. Got it?"

I nodded my head as our eyes locked onto each other. My heart was racing at the speed of light and my body temperature was on full heat. He pounded into me like I had never been before and I loved it. I wanted him to take me as hard as he could.

"Are you ready?" he asked.

"Yes," I breathlessly spoke as my body released itself to him.

His thrusting slowed as he moaned and then he pushed one last time deep inside, filling me up with his come. He lowered his head and brushed his lips against mine before collapsing on top of me and wrapping his arms securely around my neck. We lay there, trying to catch our breath and taking in the pleasure we both had given each other.

He rolled off of me and lay on his back. Rolling on my side, I ran my hand along his chest.

"You okay?" I smiled.

"Fantastic. How about you?"

"I'm great. I bet you thought you'd never have sex in this place again."

"No. Never." He chuckled.

I glanced over at the clock. It was seven.

"It's only seven o'clock. Now what?" I asked.

"Do you want me to go?"

"No. I don't."

"If you're hungry, we can order in."

"We could but that kind of poses a problem."

"What problem is that?"

"I don't have any dishes or silverware. I hadn't had a chance to get all that yet."

"Well, the stores don't close for another two hours. Let's go buy you some dishes."

"Now?" I scrunched up my face.

"Why not? It'll be fun. Where do you want to go?"

"I don't know. I never shopped for dishes before."

"Hold on a second." He got up and took his phone from his pants pocket. "Hey, Jane. Where's a good place to go to buy dishes and silverware? Great. Thank you. I'll explain later. Jane said to go to Bed Bath & Beyond."

"And who is Jane?" I asked.

"She's my housekeeper." He smiled as he pulled on his pants.

"Ah. Yes. You would have a housekeeper."

"I do and I love her."

I couldn't help but laugh at the cute expression on his face. Climbing off the bed, I got dressed and we headed out the door to Bed Bath & Beyond.

Chapter Twenty-One
Drew

We were walking through Bed Bath & Beyond, heading over to the section where the dishes were on display when, out of the corner of my eye, I spotted Jess.

"Ah, shit!"

"What's wrong?" Jillian asked.

"I just saw Jess over there."

"Oh. That's not good." She opened her purse and put on her sunglasses.

"What are you doing?"

"Going incognito. She would never think I was here, so I'm sure she wouldn't recognize me." We should stay at a distance from each other in case she sees you. I don't want a scene being caused."

"True. Fuck." I shook my head.

Jillian walked ahead of me and I followed behind. Once we made it to where the dishes were, we stayed at a distance. Good thing we did because I saw Jess walking towards me.

Shit. Shit. Shit. This wasn't going to be pretty.

"Well, well. What in the world are *you* doing here?" she asked as her eyes narrowed at me.

"I don't think that's any of your business, Jess. But if you must know, I'm looking to buy some new dishes."

"Why? And wouldn't Jane do that for you?"

"I like to pick out my own dishes. Now if you'll excuse me."

"Don't you want to know why I'm here?"

"Not particularly. No."

"Too fucking bad, Drew. I'm going to tell you anyway." Her voice began to get loud. "I'm here buying new bedding because I can't sleep on the ones you slept on. It makes me sick."

I arched my brow at her. "Okay. While you're it, why don't you just go and buy a whole new bed?"

I heard Jillian snicker from a few feet away.

"Maybe I will, and for the record, you're a total asshole. The next time we run into each other, do me a favor and don't approach me."

"You're the one who came over here. Not me. I have no interest in speaking to you ever again."

"Ugh." Tears started to fill her eyes. "Enjoy your boring pathetic life."

"I will. Don't you worry about that."

She turned on her heels and pushed her cart down the aisle as fast as she could. I watched as she stood in line, waiting for the next available cashier.

"Sorry you had to witness that," I spoke as I turned to Jillian.

"No worries. She's still broken up over you."

"Too bad. She needs to move on."

"I have a feeling that getting over you isn't easy." She smirked.

Giving her a small smile, I kissed the side of her head. "Let's get you some dishes and get the hell out of here."

When we arrived back at her apartment, I helped her unpack and put the dishes in the cupboard.

"Why are you putting them over there?" I asked.

"Because this is where I want them." She smiled.

"But it's more convenient for them to be placed in this cupboard."

"I'm sorry, but do you live here still?"

I sighed. "Sorry. Old habits. We haven't eaten since lunch and I'm starving. How about we go eat at that little Chinese restaurant down the street?"

"Sounds good to me."

She had her laptop sitting on the counter and a call came through.

"I have to get this. It's Kellan and we've been playing phone tag today."

"Who's Kellan?"

"My best friend. You'll see."

She accepted the call and his face appeared on the screen.

"Hey, Jilly Bean. Where the hell have you been all day?"

"Here and there. There's a few things I need to tell you, but now isn't a good time."

"Why?"

"I'm with someone right now," she spoke.

"Hmm. Just by you saying 'someone' indicates that it's of the male species. Because if it was Kristen, you would have said you were with her. Who is he, Bean? Let me see?"

She looked across the room at me and then turned her laptop around.

"Drew, meet Kellan. Kellan meet Drew."

I gave him a wave and a smile. "Nice to meet you."

He stared at me as if he was at a loss for words. Jillian must have told him about me from Hawaii.

"Nice to meet you too, Drew. Jillian Kathryn Bell. What is going on?"

"How funny is it that Drew lives in New York too? Okay, got to go, my love. We're heading out to dinner."

"Wait! Don't you dare end the call. I want details!" he shouted.

"Tomorrow. Bye, Kel." She ended the call.

I couldn't help but laugh. "Jilly Bean?" I asked.

"Pet name. He loves me. He's been calling me that since we were thirteen years old."

"It's cute. I like it." I winked.

"Don't you dare, Mr. Westbrook."

She grabbed her purse and we walked down to the Chinese restaurant.

****

Jillian

As we were sitting in the restaurant eating, Drew asked me to tell him about Kellan. So I did.

"He's the best friend anyone could ever have. The things he did for me. Wow."

"What did he do for you?" he asked.

I swallowed hard. "Drew, I'm a terrible person." I looked down in shame.

"No you're not. Don't say that." He reached across the table and placed his hand on mine.

"No, actually, I am. Remember when I told you that I booked the flight to Hawaii for a 'just in case' I decided to leave Grant?"

"Yeah. I remember."

"I had it planned all along."

His brows furrowed. "What do you mean?"

"I purposely waited for that day to leave him. It was the perfect plan and Kellan went to great lengths to help me."

"Why?" he asked in confusion.

"Because I wanted revenge on him and my parents for what they did to me. Mostly my parents. But Grant had it coming. I already told you that he was a cheater and a liar."

"And how did you and Kellan plan this so meticulously?" Drew cocked his head.

"Well." I sighed. "Where do I begin? About three months before the wedding, I placed an ad under an alias name on Craig's List for my wedding dress to be shipped out the day after my wedding."

"Did you sell it?"

"Yeah. A nice woman in Wisconsin who couldn't afford a wedding dress bought it for $50." I smiled. "A fifteen-thousand-dollar wedding dress for fifty bucks. Patricia would be so pissed."

Drew picked up his glass and took a sip of his drink. "Look at it this way. You made someone who couldn't afford a wedding dress feel like a queen." He smiled.

"I guess. So all in all, some good came out of what I did. A couple of days before the wedding, Kellan went and bought me a new phone and he rented a hotel room."

"Why the hotel room?"

"That's where I kept my luggage for my one-way ticket out of Seattle, which by the way, Kellan purchased for me. Before I left the church, I called a cab from my old phone and had him meet me at Pier 59. I did a factory reset and set it on the chair next to my ring. Once I left the church, I had the limo driver take me to Pier 59 and then I climbed into the cab and took it to the hotel. I changed out of my dress, grabbed everything I needed, and hopped on a plane."

"Did you pay off the limo driver?" He smirked.

"I sure did. Except he opened his mouth to my parents, who apparently paid him more than I did."

"Ouch. What a dick."

"Yeah. Except he didn't tell my parents that I got into a cab. The next day, Kellan went to the hotel, boxed up the wedding dress, sent it off to Wisconsin, and checked out of the hotel."

"So no paper trail on your end?"

"Nope. I left all my credit cards at home and my bank account untouched."

"If it's not too personal, how are you paying for everything?"

"When my grandmother died, and I turned twenty-one, she left me four million dollars in an offshore account that was untraceable because she knew I would need it someday."

"So you literally vanished."

"Yep. I sure did." I smiled.

"Remind me never to cross you." He winked.

"They made me that way, Drew. I'm not really that person. I just needed to escape and find me. Not the Jillian Bell they made."

"I understand. You did what you had to do. That doesn't make you a bad person."

"Thanks. But somehow I still feel like it does."

"Come on. I'm going to take you home now. It's getting late and I have an early meeting."

As soon as Roland pulled up to my building, Drew walked me up to my apartment.

"Thank you for making my shitty day a little less shitty."

"It was my pleasure." He placed his thumb on my chin. "I'm happy you're here." He leaned in and brushed his lips against mine.

"Good night, Jillian."

"Good night, Drew."

He turned and began to walk down the hallway. Pulling my phone from my purse, I dialed his number and watched as he answered his phone.

"Drew Westbrook."

"Hi. Now you have my number."

He turned around as his lips gave way to a sexy smile. "Indeed I do."

Stepping inside my apartment, I headed to the bathroom and turned on the water for a hot bath. After pouring a capful of lavender-scented bubble bath, I stripped out of my clothes and climbed into the warm, soothing water. My head was a mess. My sister was dying and I was reunited with a man whom I never thought I'd see again. A man I couldn't give my heart to, even if I wanted, because I didn't know who that heart belonged to.

Chapter Twenty-Two
Drew

I hated leaving her, but I had no choice. I had to be at the office in the morning by seven, and I would have had to have gotten up really early to leave her place to come home and get ready. Today confirmed what I already knew. I was in love with Jillian Bell. This strong feeling was something I'd never felt before. I'd never felt this way about any woman I had ever dated, including my ex-fiancée. All I wanted to do was hold her tight and tell her that everything was going to be okay. What the fuck was I doing? She shouldn't be alone tonight after hearing the news about her sister. Fuck it. I went into my closet, grabbed a suit, packed a small bag, and took a cab back over to her place since I sent Roland home. Whether she needed me or not, I was going to be there.

As I stood outside her door, I took my phone from my pocket and called her.

"Hello," her soft voice answered.

"Hi. Come to your door."

"Drew?"

"Yeah. It's me."

I heard the locks unlocking and she opened the door as her phone was still pressed to her ear.

"I don't think you should be alone tonight," I spoke as I stared into her beautiful blue eyes.

"I agree." She smiled.

I slipped my phone back in my pocket and stepped inside her apartment. She took hold of my hand and led me to the bedroom. After stripping out of my clothes and setting my alarm, I climbed in where I wrapped my arms tightly around her and she snuggled against my chest. Neither of us spoke a single word. I kissed the top of her head and we both drifted off to sleep.

The annoying sound of my alarm going off woke me out of a deep sleep. Letting out a moan, I reached over and turned it off. Jillian stirred and opened her eyes.

"Good morning." Her lips gave way to a sleepy smile.

"Good morning. Go back to sleep. I'm just going to take a shower and get ready for work. I promise to be quiet."

"Nah. I'm good. I'll go make us some coffee while you're in the shower." Her lips pressed against my chest.

"You don't have to, Jillian."

"I want to, Drew. Now shush up and go take your shower."

"If you insist, Madame." I rolled on top of her and kissed her soft lips.

After getting out of the shower, I wrapped a towel around my waist and walked to the kitchen.

"Here you go, sir. One fresh cup of coffee in a brand new stylish mug compliments of Bed Bath & Beyond."

I chuckled. "Thank you. If you don't mind, I'm going to take it in the bathroom with me so I can finish getting ready for work."

"I don't mind at all. I'll take mine back to bed with me."

She climbed into bed while I shaved in the bathroom.

"So tell me how it felt to take a shower in your old shower."

"Weird," I replied. "What are your plans for today?"

"Kristen is getting out of the hospital, so I'm going to spend the day with her."

"Good idea."

"Anything exciting going on at work today?" she asked.

"If you consider spending the day in meetings, then yes. The day will be filled with excitement."

Once I finished shaving, I walked into the bedroom and stared at Jillian as she sipped her coffee and checked her phone. God she was so beautiful and my cock was starting to get hard just looking at her. I'd never wanted to make love to anyone like I wanted to with her. Fuck it. I walked over to the nightstand, picked up my phone, and called Lia.

"It's me. I'm running late this morning, so tell Harrison I'll be there soon. I have some business to take care of first before I head into the office." I smiled at Jillian.

"And what kind of business would that be?" Jillian asked.

"Oh, I think you know exactly what I'm talking about." I removed my towel and climbed on the bed.

****

Jillian

"Can I see you later?" Drew asked as I walked him to the door.

"I don't know. It depends on Kristen."

"I understand." He kissed me. "Call me later, okay?"

"Okay." I smiled.

As I poured myself another cup of coffee, a call came through on my laptop.

"Good morning, Bean. I was hoping you were up. I take it your guest spent the night since I didn't hear from you."

"He sure did." I smiled as I leaned over the counter with my hands tightly wrapped around my coffee mug.

"How fucking freaky is this whole thing?"

"You haven't heard the freakiest part yet." I bit down on my bottom lip.

"Oh my God, tell me."

"The apartment I'm renting is his old apartment. He's my freaking landlord."

"Shut the fuck up! You're lying."

"I swear on my grandmother's grave." I held up two fingers.

His jaw dropped and he was speechless. "Okay, Jill, this is all too weird. Like crazy universe shit weird."

"I know, right? Anyway, I have something to tell you." My light mood turned somber.

"What's wrong?"

"The chemo and radiation hasn't helped Kristen and the cancer has spread. She's dying, Kel. The doctors gave her six to nine months." Tears filled my eyes.

"Jesus, Jill. I'm so sorry. I can be on the next flight to New York."

"It's okay. Just come this weekend like planned. I know with work and everything, it's hard."

"Fuck. Are you okay? Of course you're not. That was a stupid question."

"I'm hanging in there. In fact, I'm getting ready to head to the hospital."

"All right, go. I'll talk to you later and I want to hear all about Hawaii guy. I thought you said you're in a man-free zone. I knew it wouldn't last." He smirked.

"I'll be honest with you, Kel. I don't know what the fuck I'm doing. My head has so much shit going through it right now."

"Maybe you need to go talk to a shrink or something."

"Maybe I do. I'll talk to you later." I blew him a kiss.

"Bye, Bean."

Kellan was right. Maybe I did need to talk to someone. Grabbing my phone from the counter, I sent Noah a text message.

"Morning. When is Kristen being released?"

"Morning, Jill. We're on our way home now. She wants to see you."

"Tell her I'm on my way."

Chapter Twenty-Three
Drew

As I stepped into the conference room, Harrison and Lance both glared at me.

"You're late, Drew. You know how I hate to be kept waiting," Harrison spoke.

No one and nothing was going to ruin my good mood today.

"Well, Harrison, some things are worth being late for." I smirked as I took a seat across from him.

"Is that so? Then maybe there's another company out there that would respect my time and the contract to my new software program."

I sighed. "If that's how you feel, then you're free to leave."

"Hold up a second," Lance interjected and shot me a look.

Harrison narrowed his eyes as he stared at me. Or should I say glared at me.

"I'm serious, Harrison. If me being late has you all hot and bothered, then maybe you should find another company for your software. But I will tell you this; you came to us for a reason. This is my company and I decide whom I want to do business with, and right now, I don't care for your attitude. You think your software is unique? I can find someone else with something just as good, so it's no skin off my back."

"Drew!" Lance snapped.

Harrison sat there, contemplating his next words.

"You know what, Drew, I like you. You have balls and balls is what I need for my company. So let's get started, shall we?"

After our meeting ended and the contracts were signed, I shook Harrison's hand and walked him to the door.

"What the fuck was that all about?" Lance asked. "And why were you late?"

"She's here." I smiled as I grabbed the contracts and headed back to my office.

"Who's here?" Lance asked as he followed behind.

"Jillian. The girl I met on the plane and spent some time with in Hawaii."

"Huh? She's here in New York?"

"Yes. We ran into each other yesterday on the street. We had lunch, talked, did some shopping, and I don't think I need to tell you what happened next."

"So you were late because you had sex with her this morning?"

"Yep." I took a seat behind my desk.

"Okay." He nodded his head. "That's a damn good excuse for being late. So now what? Are you two officially dating?"

"I don't know, to be honest. Remember I told you she was on that self-discovery journey? We hadn't talked about what happens next. She just found out yesterday that her sister is dying."

"Man, that sucks." He looked at his watch. "But what matters is that you were reunited with her. You're Drew Westbrook and you always get what you want. Remember that. I have to go. I have that meeting with the tech department. I'll fill you in later."

After he walked out of my office, my phone pinged with a text message from Jane.

"Mr. Drew. You didn't sleep in your bed last night and you weren't home this morning. I'm dying to know why you were going to look at dishes."

I couldn't help but laugh.

"I'll fill you in when I get home. I promise."

"You better."

I was happy. Actually, I was fan-fucking-tastic. I didn't know if I'd ever felt so good. Having her here in New York, in my apartment, was euphoric to me. I had missed her so much and I worried about her being out in the world all alone. But now, she no longer had to be alone and I was going to make sure she wasn't.

****

Jillian

When I walked into Kristen and Noah's apartment, I found Kristen sitting on the couch, drinking a cup of coffee.

"Hey." I forced a smile.

"Hey, you. Come here." She held out her arms to me. "How are you?"

Seriously? She's the one who just found out she's dying and she's asking me how I am?

"I'm okay. How are you?" I asked as I looked at the gorgeous big rock on her finger. "What the—"

"He asked me last night. Apparently, he's had this ring for a while and was going to ask me on our dating anniversary."

"Oh my God! It's gorgeous. I'm so happy for you!" I squeezed her tight.

"Thanks. Will you help me plan my wedding? We want to get married as soon as possible since I don't have much time left."

My heart. *Fuck.* The ache I felt when she said that nearly sent me into a crying fit. But she wouldn't want that, so I had to hold my composure. I'd fall apart later.

"Of course I'll help you." Tears filled my eyes. *Shit.*

"Why are you crying?" she asked with a pout.

"Because I'm so happy for you and Noah."

"But you're thinking why bother since I won't be alive for much longer," she spoke.

I couldn't believe she just said that as I placed my hands over my mouth.

"NO! I'm not thinking that at all. Why would you say that?"

A small smile crossed her lips. "Because that's what everyone will think. I love Noah more than life itself and he wants us to be married, even if it is for a short while. We've talked so much about marriage in the past and I'm not going to let fucking cancer keep me from marrying my prince charming."

"I love you, Kristen."

"I love you too. So what did you do yesterday after you left the hospital? I was worried that you hid out in your apartment and cried all day."

"You're never going to believe it. You're just not." I smiled as I slowly shook my head.

Her eye narrowed as she tilted her head to the side.

"Oh God, Jill. What did you do?"

"Well," I slowly spoke.

"Ugh. Stop it! Spit it out!" She grabbed hold of my hands.

"Yesterday after I left the hospital, I decided to take a walk. Where I was walking to, I had no clue. All I knew was that I needed to walk and I ran into someone on the street."

"Shit. Don't tell me it was Grant or your parents."

"I ran into Drew."

"Shut up!" She cupped her hands over her mouth. "Drew from Hawaii? Drew that you had sex with?"

"Yes. That would be him."

"And?"

"We had lunch, went back to my place, had sex, went to Bed Bath & Beyond to buy some dishes, went to dinner, he dropped me off at home, we said goodbye and then he came back within an hour, spent the night, and then we had sex again this morning."

"Wait. You threw me off when you said you went to Bed Bath & Beyond." She laughed.

I shrugged. "We were going to order dinner in, but I didn't have any dishes to eat on. So, we went and bought some. But wait. There's more and you're going to freak the fuck out. Are you ready?"

"Wait. Let me take in a deep breath first. Okay. Go."

"He's my landlord. I'm his tenant. Go ahead, freak the fuck out now."

"I'm sorry, what?" she asked in confusion.

"The apartment that I'm renting is his old apartment. I'm renting it from HIM."

Kristen sat there, staring at me, without even blinking.

"Just hours after you left your fiancé at the altar, you met a man on a plane to Hawaii. You ended up at the same hotel, hung out with him and his girlfriend. He breaks up with his girlfriend, you spend the day together, have sex and then say goodbye. You move to New York, unknowingly rent an apartment that belongs to that man you met on a plane to Hawaii and run into each other on the street, which neither one of you had knowledge that the other one was here. Correct?"

"Yes. Sounds about right."

"He's your soul mate, Jill. All the fucking signs are there."

"Shut up. I don't believe in soul mates."

"You don't have to believe, baby sister. The universe led you to him. You were meant to leave Grant on that very day, or else you would have left his dumb ass way before that. But no. It was that day. The day you and Drew were on the same flight to Hawaii."

"You're crazy." I smiled. "It's all a coincidence. Plus, he wasn't even supposed to be on my flight. The earlier flight he was on got cancelled due to mechanical problems, so the airlines put him on my plane."

"Ah ha!" she yelled as she pointed her finger at me. "And his seat just so happened to be next to yours. Wake up, Jill." She grabbed hold of my shoulders and lightly shook me. "Drew is the man you're supposed to be with."

I rolled my eyes. "I'm not supposed to be with anyone. I'm on a journey to find myself; to know who I am."

"Duh, and your journey led you to him."

"But I really hadn't even started my journey yet when I met him," I spoke.

"Then he is your journey. Maybe you're supposed to go on a journey with him."

"No. That's ridiculous. I need to journey alone."

"Ugh. I give up." She threw her hands up in the air.

I couldn't help but laugh. "Enough about me. Let's talk wedding!"

Chapter Twenty-Four
Drew

Before leaving the office for the night, I pulled out my phone and called Jillian.

"Hello," she answered.

A wide smile crossed my face when I heard her sweet voice.

"Hi."

"Hi."

"I was calling to see if you had any plans for tonight."

"I don't. What did you have in mind?" she asked.

"Jane is cooking a fabulous meal and I was wondering if you'd like to have dinner at my place."

"I would love to have dinner at your house."

"I can pick you up."

"I have a couple of things to do first after I leave Kristen's. Give me your address and tell me a time."

"Well, it's five o'clock now. Is seven good for you?"

"Seven is good."

"Great. The address is 132 East 71st Street. I'll see you in a couple of hours."

"See you then. Bye, Drew."

"Bye, Jillian."

YES! I silently shouted to myself and walked out of my office.

"I'm going home for the night, Lia. I suggest you do the same." I smiled.

"I have to finish these contracts first and then I'll leave."

"No need. You can finish them in the morning. Go enjoy your evening."

Her eye narrowed at me and a small smile crossed her lips.

"You're in an exceptional mood."

"I am. Aren't I?" I smirked. "Remember that woman I met in Hawaii? The one I had you check on?"

"Yes. I remember. Jillian, wasn't it?"

"Yes. She's here in New York. We ran into each other yesterday and spent some time together. Now she's having dinner with me tonight at my house."

"Aw, Drew, I'm so happy for you."

"Thanks, Lia. Have a good night." I strolled down the hallway and out of the building.

****

Walking into my townhouse, I set my briefcase down in the foyer and followed the aroma of Jane's cooking to the kitchen.

"Welcome home, Drew." She smiled.

"Thanks, Jane. How's the food coming?"

"Good. But I'm confused as to why you're having me make these thick greasy burgers. You don't normally eat stuff like this. Are you having a guy's night in with Liam or Lance?"

"No. Actually, I'm having dinner with a very special girl and her name is Jillian."

She stopped cutting up the onions and looked at me.

"You never use the words 'very special' in front of a woman's name. What's up?"

"I met her in Hawaii and we ran into each other on the street yesterday."

"Ah. So I'm going to assume the dishes question was for her?"

"Yes. Coincidentally, she is the woman who is renting my apartment and she hadn't had a chance to go buy dishes yet, so I thought I would take her."

"I'm confused. You met her in Hawaii and now she's here in New York renting your apartment?"

"Yes."

"And you like this woman?"

"Yes. I like her a lot. I can't stop thinking about her for one second."

"That's sweet. I hope she's better than Jess." She made the sign of the cross.

"Jillian doesn't even compare to that bitch. By the way, when we were in Bed Bath & Beyond last night, I ran into Jess. She was buying a new bed set because she couldn't stand the thought of sleeping on the sheets that I had slept on."

Jane rolled her eyes. "I would have told her to go buy a new bed."

I chuckled. "I did."

"Good boy." She smiled as she held up her hand for a high five. "What time is Jillian coming over?"

"Around seven."

"I'm looking forward to meeting the woman who has put such a beautiful smile on your face." She winked.

"You'll like her, Jane. She's one of a kind. I'm going to go change."

After changing out of my suit and into some casual clothes, I poured myself a drink and went into my office to look over some emails that had come in. Just as I finished answering the last one, I heard the doorbell ring. Walking over with a smile, I opened the door and, instantly, she took my breath away.

"Hi there."

"Hi." She smiled brightly.

"Come on in."

"Thank you," she spoke as she shyly stepped inside. "I brought a bottle of wine."

"Thank you, but you didn't have to do that."

"I wanted to. It's my way of saying thank you for dinner."

I took the bottle of wine and led her to the kitchen.

"Jane, I would like you to meet Jillian Bell. Jillian, this my housekeeper, friend, and chef, Jane."

"It's so nice to meet you, Jillian." Jane smiled as she reached out and grabbed both her hands.

"It's nice to meet you too, Jane."

"Dinner is just about ready, so if you two go take a seat in the dining room, I'll bring it out."

I placed my hand on the small of Jillian's back as we walked into the dining room.

"Your place is amazing." She grinned as she looked around.

"Thank you. After we eat, I'll show you around."

Just as we sat down, I heard the doorbell ring and Jane answered it. I wasn't expecting anyone, so I had no clue who it could be.

"Well, hello there, Drew." Liam grinned as he walked into the dining room.

"Liam." I nodded. I knew why he was here.

"Hello, there." He extended his hand to Jillian. "I'm Drew's friend and next door neighbor, Liam Wyatt."

"Nice to meet you, Liam. I'm Jillian Bell." She politely shook his hand.

"As in daughter of Donald Bell?" He cocked his head.

"Yes. Do you know my father?"

"We met a few months ago at a business convention. He told me you were engaged to be married."

Jillian took in a deep breath. "Well, that didn't work out."

"Are you living here in New York?" he asked.

"Yes. Actually, I'm renting Drew's apartment."

"Sweet. Welcome to the Big Apple." He grinned.

"Not to interrupt, but is there a reason you stopped by?" I asked.

"Oh. Sorry. I brought the color book with the swatches for your bathroom. I gave it to Jane."

"Thanks. I appreciate it."

Placing his hands in his pocket, he spoke, "Well, I should get going. Avery and I are having dinner with Oliver and Delilah."

"It was nice to meet you, Liam."

"Nice to meet you too, Jillian."

Getting up from my seat, I walked Liam to the front door.

"Dude. Jillian Bell? Really?"

"It's a long story, and we'll talk about it over drinks. Listen, do not mention to anyone that she's living here in New York."

"Why?" he asked in confusion.

"Because her parents don't know where she is. It's complicated. Just trust me."

"Don't worry. I won't mention it to anyone. Have a good night and I want to hear all about her." He pointed at me as he walked out the door.

"I promise to tell you everything."

I walked back to the table and Jane had just set our plates in front of us. Jillian looked up at me with a smile.

"I can't believe you had Jane make these delicious-looking burgers. That was really sweet, Drew."

"It was nothing. I knew how much you loved the one at LAX. I can guarantee these are better." I winked.

Chapter Twenty-Five
Jillian

The minute I bit into my burger, the juiciness and flavor overwhelmed me.

"Oh my God, this is so good," I spoke.

Drew chuckled. "I'm glad you like it."

That had to be one of the sweetest things anybody had ever done for me. I know it was only a hamburger, but it was the point because he knew how much I loved them.

"How's Kristen doing?" he asked.

"Oh!" I exclaimed as I wiped my mouth with my napkin. "Noah proposed to her last night. They're getting married."

"Good for them. Do they have a date in mind?"

"They want to get married in two weeks. We spent all day calling different venues and everything's booked. So we're going to try a few more places tomorrow. I know it's last minute but I have to make sure this wedding is perfect. It has to be."

"How many people are they planning on having?"

"She said about a hundred."

"I think I may know of the perfect place." He smiled as he pulled his phone from his pocket. "Lester, it's Drew Westbrook. Listen, I have a friend who is planning a rush wedding and I would like to book the room for the reception. We're looking at a couple of weeks. There will be about a hundred guests. You do have a room open for Saturday night? Put my name down and hold it. Let me talk to my friend just to confirm and I'll get back with you tomorrow. Thanks, Lester."

"Wow." I grinned. "What place are you talking about?"

"The Harmonie Club. It's a private social club that I'm a member of. In fact, Liam and his brother Oliver are also members. Talk it over with Kristen, and if you want, I can take the both of you there tomorrow to look at the place."

"You'd do that?" I asked.

"Of course. Even though I don't know your sister, she deserves to have the wedding of her dreams."

This man was too much. He was kind, thoughtful, and incredibly sweet. I had already known that from the first time I'd met him on the plane, but tonight, and what he did for Kristen and Noah, really made me fall even harder for him. Getting up from my chair, I walked over to where he was sitting, took a seat on his lap, and wrapped my arms around his neck.

"Thank you." My lips softly brushed against his.

"You're welcome." He smiled.

"I would like to see the rest of your house."

"Your wish is my command." He kissed the tip of my nose.

As we got up from the chair, Jane walked in and began clearing the table.

"You don't have to clean up, Jane. Why don't you go home?" Drew spoke.

"It's fine, Drew. I'll go home after I clean up. I don't want to leave this until tomorrow morning."

"You don't have to." I smiled. "Drew and I will clean it up."

Her brow arched as she looked at Drew. "You heard her, Jane. We'll clean up." He winked.

I thanked Jane for dinner and she headed home. Drew took hold of my hand and showed me around his nine-thousand-square-foot, six-floor townhome.

"Why does one man need all this space?" I asked.

"It's an investment. Liam and I bought our townhouses at the same time. Both were in foreclosure and we got them for a really good deal."

"Maybe I need to take some investment advice from you."

His hands firmly grasped my hips. "I'd be happy to give you investment advice." His lips gave way to a warm smile.

The fire burning inside me intensified. The way his fingers lightly pressed against the fabric of my pants and the smile that touched my soul left me wanting more of him at that very moment. I'd never wanted sex with anyone as much as I wanted it with him. Every time he was near me, it was all I could think about. I was falling, or I had already fallen. I didn't know. I was lost in him, but I was also lost inside myself. His head leaned in and his lips were mere inches from mine. There was no way I was going home tonight.

His hand left my hip and cupped the side of my face as his soft lips pressed into mine. Our tongues met with excitement and our kiss deepened. My fingers deftly unbuttoned his shirt, and when the last button was undone, Drew swooped me up in his arms and carried me up two flights of stairs to his bedroom.

"I can't get enough of you," he spoke in a low tone as he put me down, took off his pants, and stared romantically into my eyes.

Lifting my shirt over my head, I tossed it to the ground while Drew's fingers reached behind and undid my bra. His tongue immediately slid across my chest, exploring each breast with passion. To be touched by any part of him was exciting and the vibrations down below were out of control. Taking his hand, I slid it down the front of my pants, desperate for his touch. His smile grew as he felt the wetness emerge from me. Hooking my fingers into the sides of his underwear, I pulled them down and grasped his hard cock. He gasped as his lips once again met mine. Stroking him up and down, his chest puffed and he took in a deep, exhilarating breath.

"I want you so badly, Jillian. I can't control myself," he spoke as he removed my hand and pushed me up against the wall.

He got down on his knees as his tongue slid down my abdomen. Gently removing my panties, he spread my legs apart and tasted the pleasure he gave me. My hands roamed through his hair and the light moans that escaped me became louder with each flick of his tongue against my clit.

"You taste so sweet and beautiful," he moaned against me. "Come for me, baby. Give me more. Give me what I desire."

His words. His moans. His mouth pressed against me and the finger he dipped inside sent me into oblivion with an orgasm I'd never forget. My fingers tightened around his head and my legs stiffened, giving him what he wanted. Standing up, he grabbed my ass and lifted me up against the wall. My weary legs wrapped tightly around him as he thrust into me, moving in and out at a rapid pace.

"Fuck, you feel so good," he whispered against my ear.

"So do you," I spoke breathlessly as his firm grip on my ass tightened.

"Come with me, baby. I need to feel you come with me."

He didn't need to tell me since I was already there. My legs tightened themselves around his waist as another orgasm swept through me.

"That's it! That's it!" he shouted as his thrusting slowed and he exploded inside me.

Our hearts were beating in sync at the speed of light as his warm breath swept over my neck. He held on to me as if he was never letting go. Carrying me over to the bed, he lay me down, still buried deep inside, and hovered over me. His eyes stared into mine before he dipped his head and softly kissed my lips.

"Stay here with me tonight," he quietly spoke. "I don't want you to leave. I want you in my bed where I can hold you all night long."

My lips gave way to a small smile and I softly whispered, "I will."

Chapter Twenty-Six
Drew

As I stroked her soft hair, I kissed the top of her head.

"I have a charity event to attend on Friday night and I would like to know if you'd be my date."

She lifted her head from my chest and her eyes locked onto mine.

"I'd love to go with you. Where's it at?"

"The Bank Ballroom over in the Financial District. It's Connor Black's annual autism gala."

"Sounds nice." She lay her head back down. "I'll have to go buy a fancy dress. I'll look when Kristen and I go shopping tomorrow for wedding dresses. Speaking of which, I'm going to call her right now and tell her about the Harmonie Club and see if she's interested."

"Good idea, and if she is, we can go look at it tomorrow after you look for wedding dresses."

"Oh shit." She lifted her head and sat up.

"What's wrong?"

"Kellan is flying in Friday for the weekend."

"Well, he can come with us to the charity event."

"Are you sure?"

"Of course." I smiled.

"Thank you." She leaned over and kissed me. "I'll ask him."

I couldn't resist. Pulling her on top of me, I wrapped my arms around her as my cock started to rise and press against her belly.

"I'm pretty sure I need to fuck you again." I grinned as I brushed a strand of her hair away from her face.

"I'm pretty sure you do too." She bit down on her bottom lip.

****

I moaned as the alarm went off and I fumbled to shut it down. Jillian rolled over into my arms and softly stroked my chest.

"Good morning."

"Good morning," she whispered as her body pressed tightly against mine.

"How did you sleep?" I asked.

"Great. How about you?"

"Great as well."

Kissing the top of her head, I climbed out of bed. "You can sleep in as late as you want. I'm going to take a shower and get ready for work."

"I'm up." She stretched.

"Okay then. Get that hot ass of yours in the shower with me."

"Mhmm. It would be my pleasure." She threw the sheet off her, exposing her sexy naked body.

After one of the longest showers I had ever taken, Jillian slipped into one of my t-shirts and called Kellan while I got dressed. Heading downstairs, I greeted Jane in the kitchen with a smile.

"Good morning, Jane."

"Good morning, Drew. I see Jillian stayed the night."

"How do you know that? She hasn't been down yet," I spoke as she handed me a cup of hot coffee.

"Her purse is right over there." She winked. "I like her, Drew. Even though I just briefly talked to her last night, I have to say, she's perfect."

"She is perfect, Jane."

"Good morning, Jane." Jillian smiled as she took a seat next to me at the island.

"Good morning, Jillian. Coffee?"

"Yes. Please."

"Thank you again for cleaning up last night," Jane spoke as she poured coffee into Jillian's cup.

"You're welcome. It was my pleasure."

"Excuse me. What about me? I helped clean up," I growled.

"Of course you did." Jillian leaned over and kissed my cheek.

Jane laughed and patted my hand. "Thank you, Drew."

After finishing our breakfast, I put on my suitcoat and Jillian walked me to the door.

"Call me later," I spoke as I kissed her goodbye.

"I will. I'm going to get dressed, head over to my place to change clothes, and then go to Kristen's."

"Sounds good." I placed my thumb on her chin. "I really enjoyed last night and in the shower this morning." I smiled.

"Me too." She bit down on her bottom lip.

Fuck. She was adorable and her beautiful face would forever be etched into my mind. I needed to leave or else I'd be picking her up and taking her back to my bed. This craving I had for her was unreal and I found it difficult to control myself around her.

"On that note, I need to leave." I winked. "I'll talk to you later."

Stepping out the door, I climbed inside the Bentley and sighed. For the first time in my entire life, I envisioned my future. It was a future that included Jillian and a life where we grow old together. It scared me to think that she wouldn't see the same future as I did and I wasn't sure if I was ready for that.

****

Jillian

Just as I entered Kristen's apartment building, Noah was on his way down.

"Morning, Jillian," he spoke as he kissed my cheek.

"Good morning. How is she today?"

"She's tired, but other than that, she says she's fine."

"Do you believe her?"

"No." He smiled. "I'm glad you're spending the day with her. Listen, I'm running late. I'll see you later."

"Oh wait!" I exclaimed as he walked away. Drew called the Harmonie Club and they have next Saturday open for the wedding. What do you think?"

"Isn't that a private club for the elite?"

"Yeah, and Drew is elite." I winked.

"Sounds good to me. I'm sure Kristen will be thrilled."

Lightly knocking on the door, I heard Kristen yell, "Come in."

"Hey, sis." I smiled as I walked to the kitchen. "How are you feeling today?"

She narrowed her eye at me and handed me a cup of coffee.

"I'm fine. Just a little tired."

"Are you sure you want to go look at dresses today? We can do it tomorrow."

"Nope. Today is the day. I'm not going to let a little bit of tiredness stop me from living the rest of my life. So tell me," she smiled as she leaned across the counter, "how was your night with Drew?"

"Amazing as always." I shyly grinned. "Listen, I have something to discuss with you."

"What's up?"

"Drew called a friend of his last night at the Harmonie Club and they have a room available for your wedding next Saturday. He said that if you're interested, he'll take us over there this afternoon so you can look at it."

"Really?" Her smile grew wide. "That was so nice of him to do that. Of course I'm interested. I can't wait to meet Mr. Drew Westbrook."

"I will let him know right now." I smiled as I pulled my phone from my purse and sent him a text message.

"Hi. Kristen would like to go look at the room."

"Excellent. I know she'll love it. I'll pick the two of you up around five o'clock. I'll call and let them know we're coming. Where do you want me to pick you up?"

"Great. I'm not quite sure where we'll be."

"Doesn't matter. Just call or text me the location and I'll be there."

"Thanks, Drew. This means a lot."

"You're welcome, Jillian. I'll see you later."

Taking a sip of my coffee, I looked at Kristen. "Drew will pick us up at five. He said just to text him the location of where we're at."

"He seems like a wonderful man."

"He is." I looked down at my cup and slowly traced the rim with my finger. "Too wonderful. You know what he did on the plane?"

"What?"

"He offered me his protein bar because I had mentioned that I was hungry. A total stranger. Grant never would have done that. He would have just eaten it in front of me."

"And that is why Grant is a fuckwad." She grinned.

"He is. Isn't he? Oh, by the way, Drew invited me and Kellan to attend a charity event on Friday night, so I'm going to need a new dress."

"Fun. You can help me pick out a wedding dress and I'll help you pick out a formal dress for the event."

"Are you sure you're up to it today?" I asked.

"Stop asking me. If I wasn't, I wouldn't go. Now come on; we have dresses to shop for."

Chapter Twenty-Seven
Jillian

The minute Kristen stepped out of the dressing room at Kleinfeld's, tears instantly filled my eyes. She looked so beautiful.

"No tears, Jill. Come on; we talked about this."

Wiping my eye, I spoke, "I'm sorry but you look so beautiful."

"I don't want to look beautiful. I want to look sexy as fuck." She smiled as she checked herself out in the mirror.

"You do."

"Nah. This dress isn't for me. Let me try on the others."

As she began to walk back into the dressing room, she stopped and turned to me.

"Why don't you try one on?"

"Who me?" I pointed to myself.

"Yes, you. Come on. Don't make me do this alone."

"No. I don't want to try on wedding dresses. I wore one for a couple of hours not too long ago. Remember?"

"Yeah. But I didn't get to see you in it."

"Trust me, you missed nothing. Besides, it'll be a cold day in hell before I ever get back into a wedding dress."

"Don't say that, Jill."

"It's true."

She shook her head and headed into the dressing room. After trying on six different dresses and not liking any of them, she stepped out in the last dress she had in the room.

"Wow," I spoke as I got up from the plush chair and walked over to her as she stared at herself in the three-way mirror.

"This is the one, Jill." Her eyes filled with tears.

Laying my head on her shoulder, I spoke, "It's perfect, Kristen."

"I have the perfect head piece for you." The saleswoman smiled.

After a few moments, she returned with a lightly beaded white satin head scarf with a veil attached to the back of it. Taking it from her hands, I placed it on Kristen's head.

"What do you think?"

"Now it's complete."

As soon as Kristen went to change out of the dress, I pulled the saleswoman to the side.

"How fast can you get this dress altered?"

"We would order her a brand new one closer to her size."

"We don't have time. She's getting married next Saturday."

"I'm sorry, but that's impossible. We send our dresses out to be altered."

"Not good enough. I need you to listen to me very carefully. My sister only has six to nine months left to live. Her cancer has spread and there's nothing more the doctors can do to help her. This wedding will be the last thing she ever does and I'm going to make sure it's perfect."

"I'm very sorry to hear that. A friend of mine is a seamstress and she owns a shop over on East 48th Street. I can give her a call for you and see what she says."

"Thank you." I smiled. "Also, I'll be paying for the dress and headpiece. I can give you a deposit today and bring in the rest of the cash tomorrow. Please let me know what your friend says. Here's my phone number."

Kristen walked out and handed the dress to the saleswoman. "I'll be putting this on my credit card," she spoke.

"No need. I'm buying you the dress."

"No, Jill. No you're not."

"Actually, I am, and there's nothing you can do about it." I grabbed both her hands and held them tight. "The mother of the bride is supposed to buy the wedding dress, but since your mom can't be here, your sister is the next best thing."

"Jill." Tears formed in her eyes.

"I want to do this for you. So let me."

She let go of my hands and wrapped her arms around me.

"Thank you. I don't know what to say."

"You're welcome and you don't need to say anything."

"Excuse me," the saleswoman interrupted our sisterly moment. "My friend, Gina, said she'd be more than happy to alter the dress for you. She said you can come now if you would like and she'd get started on it right away."

"Thank you."

"No problem. By the way, the dress rang up on clearance." She winked at me. "Your deposit was enough to cover it."

"Thank you." I gave her a light hug.

She bagged up the dress and we hailed a cab over to Gina's Seam Shop over on East 48th Street. After we met with Gina, I could tell Kristen was exhausted.

"I'm starving," I spoke. "Let's go sit down and grab some lunch."

"Sounds good to me. Where do you want to go?"

"I'm new to this city, so you pick."

We ended up taking a cab over to SoHo and eating at a place called Balthazar. As I was taking a bite of my chicken club sandwich, I almost choked on it when I saw Jess walking over to the table.

"Jillian?" She cocked her head as a look of disbelief swept over her face.

"Jess. Oh my God." I stood up and gave her a light fake hug.

"What are you doing here?" she asked.

"Having lunch."

"I mean in New York."

"I live here now."

"I thought you were on a self-discovery journey."

"I am."

"Does Drew know you're here in New York?" Her eyes shot back at me.

Shit. Shit. Shit. What do I say? It was none of her fucking business and I had nothing to hide.

"Yes. I ran into him the other day. He was just as surprised as you are right now."

"I'm sure he was. Well, it was nice seeing you again. Maybe we can do lunch some time."

"That would be great," I lied. There was no way in hell I would have lunch with her.

As soon as she walked away, Kristen leaned over the table.

"Who the fuck was that snobby bitch?"

"Drew's ex-girlfriend."

"The one he dumped in Hawaii?"

"Yep. She's the one." I rolled my eyes.

After finishing lunch, Kristen couldn't stop yawning.

"Why don't I see if Drew can take us to the Harmonie Club now? You really need to get home and lie down."

"I am really beat." She sighed.

Taking my phone from the table, I sent Drew a text message.

"I'm sorry to bother you because I know you're busy, but would it be possible to go look at the Harmonie Club now? Kristen is exhausted and I'm afraid she won't make it until five o'clock."

"Of course. I just finished lunch. Where are you?"

"A restaurant called Balthazar."

"Ah. One of my favorite places. I'll be there in about twenty minutes."

"Thank you, Drew."

"I'll see you soon, baby."

I sat and stared at the last word he typed. An uneasy feeling swept over me. He called me "baby" during sex, which was acceptable because it was spoken in the midst of hot steamy sex. But for him to call me that while not having hot steamy sex didn't sit right with me.

"What's wrong?" Kristen asked. "Did he say no?"

"No. He said he's on his way."

"Okay. What's the look for then?"

"It's just he called me baby."

"Aw, that's sweet, Jill. Why does that bother you?"

"Because we're not in a relationship. Names like that are reserved for couples. Not for two people who are friends."

Narrowing her eye at me from across the table, she spoke, "You mean two people who are having a lot of sex and spending the nights with each other."

"We aren't in a relationship."

"Actually, you are. You're in a sexual relationship. If you don't want to be in any kind of relationship with him at all, then you need to stop fucking him." She graciously smiled.

"What if I don't want to? He makes me feel incredible and sex with him is very addicting."

"Then stop getting all pissed off when he calls you baby. You can't have your cake and eat it too, Jill. I have a feeling that Mr. Drew Westbrook wants more from you than just a sexual relationship."

"That's too bad. I've made it very clear to him that I'm not interested in a relationship."

She sighed. "Okay. Okay. Let's go wait outside."

Just as we stepped out the doors of Balthazar, Drew's Bentley pulled up to the curb and Roland stepped out and opened the door for us.

"Hi." I smiled as I climbed in next to Drew.

"Hi." He grabbed hold of my hand.

Kristen climbed in and I immediately introduced them.

"Drew, this is my sister, Kristen. Kristen, meet Drew Westbrook."

"Hello, Kristen. It's nice to finally meet you."

"Likewise, Drew. Thank you for doing this for us."

"No problem. It's my pleasure to help you in any way I can. How was your lunch?"

"Lunch was good. The food was great and I ran into someone I know." I smirked.

"Really? Who?"

"Jess."

"Fuck. What did she say?" He slowly shook his head.

"She wanted to know why I was in New York and then asked me if you knew I was here."

Rolling his eyes, he sighed. "What did you tell her?"

"That you knew because we ran into each other and then she said we should do lunch some time."

"You're not going to, are you?"

"Of course not. Why would I?"

Roland pulled up to the Harmonie Club and the three of us climbed out and went inside. Drew told the lady at the desk to alert Lester that we had arrived.

"Good to see you, Drew." Lester smiled as they shook hands. "Follow me and I'll show you what's available."

He took us up to the third floor where the Harmonie Room was located.

"Take a look around and let me know what you think. This room holds up to three hundred and fifty guests very comfortably. If you're interested in having the ceremony here, we can accommodate you in the main dining room for an additional fee and you're free to decorate it how you wish."

"Thank you, Lester. We'll let you know."

Giving Drew a pat on the back, he stepped out of the room while we looked around.

"Wow. This is beautiful," Kristen spoke. "I'm afraid to ask how much this would cost." She bit down on her bottom lip.

"Don't worry about the cost, Kristen," Drew spoke. "Being a member, I get a discount." He winked.

After looking around, Kristen agreed to have the reception and ceremony at the Harmonie Club. Things were coming together and I couldn't be happier for her. After we climbed back into the Bentley, Roland drove us back to Kristen's apartment.

"Are you coming up?" she asked me.

"I think I'm going to head home. You, my tired sister, need to go take a long nap."

"True." She smiled. "Call me later." She leaned over and kissed my cheek. "Thank you again, Drew. You are a lifesaver."

"You're welcome. I'm happy you liked it."

Chapter Twenty-Eight
Drew

After Kristen climbed out and shut the door, I placed my hand on Jillian's cheek and stole a kiss.

"I've been waiting to do that." I grinned.

A light smile crossed her beautiful plump lips. "Thank you."

"Can I see you later? I can come by your place and bring dinner."

"I was going to take a bath."

"You can take a bath."

The thought of her in the bathtub aroused me.

"What if I'm in the tub when you arrive and I can't let you in."

"I have a key. I can let myself in." I winked.

She laughed and laid her head on my shoulder.

"Then by all means, Mr. Westbrook, come on over."

After dropping Jillian off at home, I headed to the office. As I was walking down the hallway, I stopped when I saw Jess standing in front of Lia's desk.

"What the hell is going on here?" I asked as I glared at Jess.

"Oh. So you weren't in your office. I thought your secretary was lying to me."

I sighed. "What do you want, Jess?" I walked into my office.

"I ran into somebody today at lunch."

"And I care why?" I raised my brow at her.

"I ran into Jillian. Remember her? The girl you met on the plane to Hawaii? The girl we had dinner with?"

"Okay. And?"

"She told me she ran into you the other day."

"Yes. So?"

"Are you dating her?"

"No. I'm not dating her. And even if I was, what business is it of yours? What part of 'we're over' do you not understand?"

"I know we're over, asshole. My point is that I think you have a thing for her and I believe that's why you broke up with me."

Rolling my eyes, I leaned back on my desk.

"I broke up with you because you are a selfish woman, Jess. Now I refuse to get into this again with you. I have work to do. Please leave and don't come back here again."

"What happened to you?" She glared at me. "You've changed so much since we first met."

"Maybe it was the toxic people in my life that changed me. You being the toxic person. If you want, I can call security and have them escort you out."

"I hate you, Drew Westbrook."

"So you've said a million times. If you hate me so much, why do you still come around? Don't you see how pathetic that is?"

"I'm leaving." She turned on her heels and headed towards the door. "And for the record, I really do hate you." She slammed the door shut behind her.

It wasn't too long before Lia knocked on the door and stepped inside.

"Are you okay, Drew?"

"Of course." I smiled. "I can honestly say that I have never been better."

After finishing up some work, I had Roland stop by my townhouse so I could pack a small overnight bag. I had every intention of spending the entire night with Jillian. On the way to her apartment, I stopped by the florist and picked her up a small bouquet of lilies. I desperately wanted to get her roses, but I thought that roses right now wouldn't be appropriate.

Entering her apartment, I called out to her.

"I'm in the bathtub."

A smile crossed my lips because seeing her naked body right when I walked through the door was what had been on my mind all day long. Walking into the bathroom, I leaned against the doorframe, holding the lilies in one hand and a bottle of Prosecco in the other.

"Hi." Jillian smiled as she lay there in a tub full of bubbles with her hair twisted up in a clip.

"Hi." I held up the flowers and Prosecco.

"You shouldn't have."

"I wanted to." I stared intently into her blue eyes.

"Thank you. There's a vase in the cabinet in the living room."

"I'll be right back," I spoke.

I placed the flowers in a vase of water and opened the Prosecco, pouring some into two wine glasses.

"Here you go," I handed Jillian her glass and set mine down on the bathroom counter.

Kneeling down on the floor in front of the tub, I took the loofah sponge sitting on the edge and began softly rubbing it across her shoulders.

"I forgot to ask you. Did you and Kristen find a wedding dress today?"

"Yes, and the lady at the bridal shop called a friend of hers that is a seamstress and she's going to do the alterations."

"Good. I'm happy it's all working out for her."

"Yeah. Me too." She brought her hand up to her face and wiped her eye.

"What's wrong?"

"Everything." A tear fell down her cheek.

"Talk to me, Jillian."

"God, I feel like such an idiot right now for crying in front of you like this."

"Don't feel that way. You're not an idiot and I think you're beautiful when you cry."

She let out a light laugh. "Thanks."

I stood up, kicked off my shoes, and climbed in the tub with her.

"What are you doing?" She grinned.

"Comforting you the proper way." I wrapped my arms around her and pulled her in to me. "We'll sit in here for as long as you need."

Chapter Twenty-Nine
Jillian

I couldn't believe he climbed into the bathtub in his clothes. My arms were wrapped tightly around his neck as my head lay on his shoulder.

"Everything is happening so fast and before you know it, she'll be gone. To be honest, I don't know how I'm ever going to get over that."

"You'll never get over it. But as each day passes, you'll heal and you'll accept it and you'll move on with your life holding on to the memories that the two of you shared."

Lifting my head from his shoulder, I stared into his eyes.

"It sounds like you've lost someone before."

"I have. My best friend, Scott, was killed in a car accident when he was sixteen years old. It really hit me hard because we were like brothers. He was an only child like me. We went to school together and had planned to go to MIT together. We hung out every day working on projects, playing basketball, working out, and just talking about life and our future. We had this plan to backpack through Europe the summer we graduated high school."

"I'm sorry." I hugged him tight. "He'd be so proud of you and what you've accomplished at such a young age."

"I know. You'll survive, Jillian. I know it's unfair that this shit is happening to Kristen at such a young age, but you'll be okay, and after you've grieved, you'll be able to smile at the things that remind you of her."

"I'm worried about Noah. He loves her so much and I don't know how he's going to get through it."

"You'll help each other get through it and I'll be here to pick you up when you fall and I'll be here when you smile again."

I pressed my lips into the side of his neck. I had never felt so supported as I did at that moment.

"We should get out of the tub now."

"Good idea." He smiled as he kissed my lips.

Drew climbed out first, grabbed a towel, held it open for me, and wrapped it around my body when I got out of the tub.

"You better get out of those wet clothes. Did you bring extra, by any chance?" I smirked as I unbuttoned his shirt.

"I may have."

"Did you bring food?"

"No. We'll order in. We can do that now that you have plates and silverware."

"Good. I don't feel like going out."

"I don't either."

"So a casual night in it is." I smiled as I walked out of the bathroom.

After changing into my cotton cami and matching short pajamas, I walked to the kitchen and took in the scent of the beautiful lilies Drew gave me.

"These smell so pretty." I smiled as he walked in wearing a pair of sweatpants and a t-shirt. He was just as sexy and hot dressed down as he was in his suits.

"I'm happy you like them. Now, what's for dinner?" He placed his hands firmly on my hips from behind.

"Whatever you're in the mood for. I really don't care. I like just about anything."

"How about Mediterranean?"

"Mhmm. Sounds good to me."

Drew pulled up the menu on his phone for a Mediterranean place a couple of blocks away. I took a sip of my wine as I stood and stared at him while he placed our order. I didn't want to admit to myself that I enjoyed this. Him. His company. Us, in our pajamas, ordering in food was something that relaxed me. He relaxed me, and being with him made me feel things I'd never felt before. I couldn't explain it. I was myself and I didn't need to hide behind the mask that had become attached to me for a better part of my life. I didn't need to pretend to be happy. I could be sad and he'd be there to hold me and tell me that it was okay. I couldn't do that with my parents. The moment a tear fell from my cheek, my mother would place her finger under my chin and tell me that Bell women didn't cry and that it was a sign of weakness. If I cried in front of Grant, all I would get was, "Why are you being so hormonal?" So I learned not to cry. But the day I left my family was the day the tears started to come back without shame.

"Are you okay?" Drew asked as he placed his phone on the counter.

"Yeah." I smiled.

"How about we watch a movie while we eat," I spoke, placing my hand on his chest.

"Okay. What do you want to watch?"

"I don't know. Let's see what's on."

I took hold of his hand and led him over to the couch. Picking up the remote, I turned on the TV and searched under the movie section.

"We can do sappy, thriller, comedy. It's your choice." I smiled.

"Nope. I picked what we're having for dinner. So it's only right you pick what we watch."

"Oh look. *Magic Mike* is available." I grinned as I looked to see his reaction.

"*Magic Mike*, eh? Never saw it. So if that's what you want to watch, then turn it on."

Narrowing my eye at him, I spoke, "Really? Are you sure?"

"I told you that it was your pick."

Just as I clicked "watch," there was a knock at the door.

"Saved by the knock." Drew winked and I playfully smacked his ass as he walked away.

Drew grabbed two plates and brought the food over to the couch. I pressed play and the movie began. This was one movie I would never grow tired of. We ate and finished off the bottle of Prosecco while we watched the movie.

"You like when he does that?" he asked as he pointed to Channing Tatum.

"Maybe." I chewed on my bottom lip.

Drew got up from the couch and stood in front of the TV. He pulled his t-shirt over his head and tossed it on the floor while his hips moved back and forth. Cupping my hands over my mouth, I smiled in delight and could feel my panties getting wetter by the second. His tongue swept over his lips as he seductively moved towards me. Hooking his fingers in the waistband of his sweatpants, he slowly took them down with a smile. I had never been so turned on as I watched him dance in front of me. He approached me and took my hand, lifting me from the couch, grinding his body against mine as his eyes stared into mine.

"Perfect." I smiled. "Thank you for the show."

"Oh, baby, it's not over yet." His lips pressed against mine. "It doesn't stop here." He swooped me up in his arms and twirled me around, then carried me to the bedroom.

****

The riveting feeling that flooded my body from my third orgasm seemed to stay with me longer than it should have. Some serious mind-blowing sex had just taken place and left me feeling breathless. His fingers lightly swept over my ass as he held me under the sheets.

"You're something else, Mr. Westbrook." I softly stroked his arm.

"Thank you, Miss Bell. I aim to please and I hope my performance went way beyond your expectations."

"Oh, it definitely did." I laughed. "Way beyond."

I should have been happy as I lay there in his arms, but something took its place. It wasn't sadness, but confusion. What was I confused about? I had this generous, kind, loving, sexy-as-fuck man who was attracted to me and wanted me. He occupied every area of my body and mind. He comforted me. He gave me strength when I thought I already had it and he was there for me in more ways than one. Even when he didn't know me from Adam on the plane, he was there for me. I wanted to love him, and a part of me already did. But there was another part of me, deeper inside, that told me no. It was the stranger that I saw in the mirror every day.

Chapter Thirty
Jillian

Friday had come and Kellan had to cancel his flight to New York because he was sick with a 102 fever and a bad cough. When he skyped me, I knew the moment he appeared on the screen something was wrong. He had been sick for a couple of days but didn't feel the need to tell me because he thought he'd get better. Stepping out of the shower and wrapping a towel around me, I walked into my bedroom and stared at the long red, sleeveless, deep v neckline, with a cut out back evening gown I was going to wear tonight to the charity event.

"So, are you excited about tonight?" Kristen asked me as she stood in the doorway holding a glass of water.

"I think it'll be fun."

"You hate these things."

"I hated them with my parents and Grant. I'll be with Drew, so it'll be fun." I walked into the bathroom and started applying my makeup.

"You're in love with him. I can tell. You don't have to hide it from me."

"I'm not hiding anything and I'll admit, I do like Drew."

She cocked her head at me as she sat down on the toilet.

"He's a good man, Jill, and I know he loves you. I can tell just by the way he looks at you."

"Maybe it's lust on both our parts. He doesn't want marriage. I don't want marriage. So why get heavily involved? If I wanted marriage, I would have married Grant." I shuddered.

She sighed. "You never loved Grant to begin with and the marriage was just a way to get revenge on your parents. You knew you'd never go through with it. But it's different with the man you love."

"I'm not in love, Kristen. I need to love myself and the person I am before I can love another."

"Well, I love you for the person you are and you can't tell me otherwise."

I looked over at her with a small smile. "I love you too."

"I have a feeling Mr. Westbrook is going to get his heart broken."

I didn't reply to her comment. After my makeup was applied, I curled the ends of my hair and pinned my sides back into an elegant style. Slipping into my dress, I stared at myself in the mirror.

"You look sexy." Kristen smiled. "I hope you have matching panties on underneath that dress.

"I do." I winked.

"Oh, by the way, Noah and I mailed out the invitations today and I posted a 'save the date' on Facebook. I apologized to everyone for the short notice, but time isn't exactly on my side."

I hated when she said things like that and a sick feeling emerged in the pit of my stomach.

"Everyone will be there, and it's going to be fabulous."

"I'm going to head out before Drew gets here." She kissed my cheek. "Have fun tonight and I want all the details in the morning. That's if you and Drew can manage to drag yourselves out of bed."

I laughed. "I'll call you tomorrow."

Just as she was about to leave, I heard Drew's voice. As I walked into the living room, he stopped talking to Kristen and stared at me with a smile splayed across his face.

"Wow. You look gorgeous."

"Thanks. So do you." I smiled. "Look at that tux." I walked over and placed my hand on his chest.

"Are you ready?"

"I am. Just let me grab my purse."

"My mom called today and asked me over for a dinner tomorrow. I would love for you to come with me. I mentioned you to her."

"What did you say?"

"I just told her that I met a beautiful woman and I would like them to meet you."

"Parents. That's a big step." I grinned.

"Nah. They're cool. Don't think of them as my parents. Just think of them as people I know."

"Okay. A barbeque sounds great. I'd love to go with you."

****

"Wow, look at this turnout," I spoke as we walked arm in arm into the Bank Ballroom.

"Connor's events are always successful."

As a waiter walked by holding a tray of champagne, Drew grabbed two glasses and handed me one. We mixed and mingled with his business associates and friends.

"I'm going to go find the restroom," I spoke as I placed my hand on Drew's arm.

"Okay. I'll wait right here."

Giving him a smile, I made my way to the bathroom. As I was sitting in the stall, the bathroom door opened and I froze when I heard a familiar voice. No. It couldn't be. I sat there, literally shaking with my heart pounding out of my chest as I listened to the two women have a conversation. My breathing had become restricted while I sat there waiting for them to leave. After I heard the door open and then close again, the bathroom became silent. Quickly leaving the stall, I washed my hands and slowly opened the bathroom door. I needed to get out of here and fast. I had no time to tell Drew I was leaving as I made a beeline down the hallway and through the ballroom as quickly as I could. There was a crowd of people gathered around listening to Connor's speech. If I could just get past them unnoticed, everything would be okay. My legs were shaking and I couldn't seem to get a hold of myself. I was almost across the room where the exit doors were located when I accidentally bumped into a man.

"Oh, excuse me, young—Jillian?" His eyes widened.

I swallowed hard. "Daddy."

He grabbed hold of my arm to prevent me from taking another step.

"My God. Have you been in New York all this time?"

"Let me go, Daddy." Tears started to fill my eyes. "Please, if you ever loved me, you'll let me go."

"There is no way I'm letting you go. What the hell happened to you?"

"There you are, dar—" My mother stopped mid-word as her eyes popped out of her head. "Jillian?"

Fuck. Fuck. Fuck.

"You have some serious explaining to do, young lady!" Her voice grew loud.

This was it. I knew one day this moment would come, but I didn't think it would be so soon. I needed to collect my thoughts and, for the first time in my life, stand up to my parents. I was a twenty-four-year-old woman with her own life and I needed to act like one. As much as I wanted to run out of the room, I would face them as an adult.

"What's going on here?" Drew asked as he walked up and saw the hold my father had on me.

"Excuse me? Who are you?" my mother asked as she looked him up and down.

"It's not important who I am. Please remove your hand from her now before I do it for you." He glared at my father.

"Drew, these are my parents."

"Oh shit," he spoke.

"Like your mother said, Jillian, you have some serious explaining to do. What kind of person does what you did?" My father asked.

"Yes. Do you know the embarrassment you have caused this family?" my mother spoke through gritted teeth. "Not to mention what you did to poor Grant. He's devastated."

My jaw dropped. "Oh yeah, poor Grant. The two-timing, lying, cheating son of a bitch!" I yelled.

"Okay. Not here." Drew placed his arm around my waist.

"Is this your new boy toy?" my mother scowled.

"I'm Jillian's friend and this is not the place to have this discussion."

"Fine," my father spoke. "We can do it in our hotel suite. We're staying at the Plaza. Jillian, come with us."

"No."

"Jillian, you heard what your father said. Now let's go!" my mother harshly spoke.

"No." I folded my arms.

"Excuse us for a moment." Drew held up his finger and took hold of my arm, leading me away from my parents. "I know you're in shock right now, but you knew eventually you'd have to face them. They're here now, so you might as well get it over with. Once you've talked, it's over."

"There is no talking to them, Drew."

"Jillian, you are twenty-four years old. They can't hurt you anymore. Tell them how you feel and move on."

"Will you come with me?"

"Of course I will." He kissed my head. "Take in a deep breath. You can do this. You're a strong, independent woman."

"Fine."

I walked over to where my parents were standing. "We'll follow you to the Plaza."

"No. You'll be coming with us. Your friend can see you another time," my mother spoke.

I glared at my mother as the rage inside started to consume me.

"I said we'll follow you to the hotel. He's coming with me or else you don't get to talk to me. Do you understand?"

"It's fine, Jillian." My father sighed. "Let's go. Shall we?"

Chapter Thirty-One
Jillian

I took in a deep breath as Drew placed his hand on the small of my back and we climbed into the Bentley.

"The Plaza Hotel, Roland," he spoke.

"I don't think I can do this sober. I need a drink. Don't you keep any liquor in here?" I asked as I looked around.

"Jillian, you'll be fine." He took hold of my hand. "Trust me. You can do this and I'll be there right by your side."

"I still need alcohol." I laid my head on his shoulder.

"I can guarantee there's a fully stocked fridge in their suite. Just grab something when you get in there."

Roland pulled up behind my parents' limo and the four of us got out at the same time. My mother glared at me the whole way up to their suite. Once the door shut, the shit was about to hit the fan. My nerves were spastic and I needed to calm down. Walking over to the refrigerator, I opened it and pulled out a bottle of beer.

"What on earth are you doing?" my mother asked in disgust as I took the cap off the bottle and took a large sip.

"I'm drinking a beer. Do you have a problem with that?"

"You better watch your attitude, young lady." My father pointed at me. "Now sit down!"

"No thank you. I'd rather stand. So, who's going to go first? Mother? Father?"

"Why did you do it?" my father asked. "After everything your mother and I have done for you, this is how you repay us?"

"And how dare you say those things about Grant," my mother chimed in. "He's heartbroken."

"I'm sure he is," I spoke in a sarcastic tone. "And to answer your question, Daddy, I did it because I wanted out."

"What do you mean by that?" he growled.

"I wanted out from the grips of both of you. You ran my entire life. You never once asked me what I wanted."

"It didn't matter what you wanted. We're your parents and we knew what was best for you," my mother said.

"No! You didn't know what was best for me," I shouted. "You never let me explore life and do the things I wanted to do. You were so busy trying to make sure I was the perfect daughter that made you look good that you didn't give a damn about how I felt."

"Oh, stop being so dramatic." My mother waved her hand in front of her face. "We gave you everything you wanted."

"You gave me everything you thought I wanted!" I pointed at her. "You chose my friends, what I ate, what I could and couldn't wear, what school I had to attend, college, my career, and my future husband! You didn't give me a choice, and like a fool, I put up with it for far too long. Grant didn't want to marry me any more than I wanted to marry him. He cheated on me! Did you know that on the night of his bachelor party, he slept with not one, but two strippers at the same time?!"

My mother looked away with a nasty look on her face. "Grant loves you. He would never do that and what you did to him and to us is unforgivable." She folded her arms.

"Well, at least we agree on something because what you did to me is unforgivable."

The room became silent for a few moments, and when I looked over at Drew, there was a deep sadness in his eyes. This wasn't fair to him. He shouldn't have had to hear this.

"You've embarrassed this family, Jillian," my father spoke. "And you threw away a million-dollar wedding."

"Is that all that matters to you? The money? I didn't ask for a fucking million-dollar wedding. That was all her," I pointed to my mother, "doing."

"Why did you come to New York?" he asked. "And how did you slip away so quietly without a trace? You haven't used your credit cards and your bank account hasn't been touched. What have you been doing for money?"

"Oh, I'm sure this one over here has been supporting her." My mother pointed at Drew. "Is that why you left Grant? For him?"

Narrowing my eyes at her, I couldn't believe she dragged Drew into this.

"How dare you! You want the truth?" I strutted over to her and my father. "Because you aren't going to like it. When I turned twenty-one, my grandmother left me a trust fund with four million dollars in it."

The shock on their faces was priceless and it gave me great satisfaction to finally tell them.

"What?" my father asked in anger.

"That's right, Daddy. Your mother made sure that I would be taken care of when I finally decided to break free from this so-called family and prison I was living in. She knew everything."

"That wretched woman!" he yelled. "How dare she hide that from me!"

"She did it because she loved me and knew I needed an out. As long as I stayed in Seattle around the two of you and Grant, I would never know who I truly was."

Seeing them sitting there weak and their defenses down gave me the strength to continue. Drew sat back in his chair, staring at me and waiting for what was to come next.

"What do you mean you would never know who you truly were?" my father asked.

"You made me into someone I don't even know! You molded me into what you wanted me to be. You didn't let me decide what I wanted to be or let me discover myself. You shoved your life down my throat and every time I look in the mirror, I see a complete stranger!"

"Oh for God's sake, Jillian. You are such a drama queen," my mother snarled. "The fact of the matter is that you have embarrassed this family and you need to do some serious apologizing. Not only to us and the community that supported you, but also to Grant."

I could feel the fire rise inside my body and the anger I felt grew more intense.

"An embarrassment? Me?" I calmly spoke. "If anyone should be embarrassed, it's you, Daddy."

"Me? Why me?"

"Do you know why I came to New York?"

My mother rolled her eyes. "I'm sure it was for him."

"LEAVE DREW OUT OF THIS!" I shouted. "I came here because of my sister! You know, the child you created with another woman?" I glared at my father.

My mother looked at him and swallowed hard while my father sat there and blankly stared at me. Finally, they were speechless.

"How did you find out about her?" my mother asked.

Cocking my head, I narrowed my eye at her. "You knew about her?"

"Of course I did. Now answer the question."

"She contacted me two years ago after her mother passed away. She told her everything. We bonded and became close like sisters should be. I can't believe I had a sister and you never told me!"

"You were never supposed to find out about her," my father softly spoke as he looked down.

"Well, too fucking bad. I did. What kind of father just ignores the fact that he has another child?"

"I'm not rehashing the past, Jillian. Drop it and you are never to speak of her to anyone."

"Well, you don't have to worry about that because she'll be dead in six to nine months." A tear formed in my eye.

My father looked up at me. "What do you mean?"

"She has brain cancer and there's nothing more the doctors can do for her. So I hope you feel like shit, but I'm sure you don't. Neither one of you has a compassionate bone in your body."

My mother raised her brow and looked away.

"I'm sorry," my father spoke.

"Sorry?" I leaned my ear towards him. "You're sorry for what? That I found out, that she's dying, or that you never got the chance to know your own daughter?"

"Maybe all of it." He looked down.

I stood there and slowly shook my head.

"I thank God every day that I'm nothing like the both of you. How I'm not is a miracle."

They both sat there in silence and Drew looked at me with a small grin. He knew I had won.

"I want to meet her," my father spoke.

"What?" my mother lashed out. "No! You are not meeting that woman."

"Will you shut the hell up for once in your life, Patricia!" he commanded at her. "I never should have listened to you in the first place. Now I've lost two daughters."

"Jillian will be coming home. We'll work this out. She'll apologize and we can all move on."

"The fuck I will!"

"Don't you dare use that language in my presence," she spoke in anger.

"Oh, I will use that language in your presence. You cannot and will not tell me what to do. I am a grown woman who makes her own decisions. If I want to say 'fuck,' I will and I'll say it as many times as I want to."

"What happened to you?" My mother narrowed her eyes in disgust at me. "What happened to my daughter?"

"The daughter you created is gone and she's never coming back. She's dead and buried deep down in the depths of the Earth. By the way, that man sitting over there that you keep referring to, his name is Drew Westbrook and you will respect him."

I grabbed my purse from the table and Drew followed me to the door.

"Goodbye, Mr. and Mrs. Bell. Oh, and by the way, Patricia, Kellan helped me plan my little escape. He knew where I was the whole time. You are to stay away from him. If I even catch a hint of you going anywhere near him again, I will leak to the press about Daddy's illegitimate child and how the two of you went to great lengths to keep her a secret."

"You wouldn't dare." She glared at me.

"And you never thought I'd skip out on my wedding day either." I smiled. "Don't underestimate me. I learned from the best."

Walking out the door, I let out a deep breath and fell into Drew's arms.

Chapter Thirty-Two
Drew

I held her as tightly as I could and ran my hand up and down her back. I expected her to break down and start crying, but she didn't.

"I'm so proud of you for holding it together in there and standing up to them." I kissed the top of her head. "Are you okay?"

She broke our embrace and looked up at me.

"I'm fine. Actually, I feel great. Is that fucked up?"

I let out a light chuckle. "I'm not sure."

"Let's get out of here before one of them opens the door," she spoke.

As we climbed into the back of the Bentley, Jillian laid her head on my shoulder.

"Will you stay with me tonight?" she asked.

"Of course I will. I wasn't planning on leaving you anyway. Where do you want to stay? My place or yours?"

"How about your place? But can we stop by mine really quick so I can grab some clothes for tomorrow? I really don't feel like putting this dress back on in the morning."

"To Jillian's apartment, Roland," I spoke.

After stopping by Jillian's apartment, we headed to my townhouse. Jillian went upstairs while I grabbed a bottle of wine and a couple of glasses. When I walked into the bedroom, she was in the bathroom washing her face and letting her hair down. I poured us some wine, climbed under the covers, and waited for her.

"I brought some wine. I figured you'd want some."

"Thank you." She softly smiled as she climbed in next to me.

Taking the glass from my hand, she brought it to her lips.

"So now what?" I asked. "What are you going to do about your parents?"

"Nothing. I said what I had to and it's done. I'm never going back to Seattle. I'm sorry you had to witness all that and I'm sorry for ruining your night."

"You didn't ruin my night and don't be sorry. Your parents. Wow." I shook my head.

"I told you. They're something else. I lived my whole life like that." She finished off her wine and held her glass to me.

Grabbing the bottle from the nightstand, I refilled her glass.

"Are you still up for going to my parents' house tomorrow?"

"Of course I am. Do you think I'm going to let this ruin anything? I'm done letting my parents ruin and run my life."

I reached over and softly stroked her cheek. "You are a brave woman, Jillian Bell."

"Thanks. I'm trying to be. Tonight was the last thing I needed with everything else going on."

"I know." I pulled her into me and kissed her head.

****

The next morning, I opened my eyes as Jillian stirred in my arms. Kissing her back, I softly spoke, "Good morning."

She turned and faced me, placing her hand and her head on my chest.

"Good morning. What time is it?"

"Eight o'clock."

She yawned.

"You were restless last night," I spoke.

"I kept having bad dreams about my parents. Ugh. I don't want to think or talk about them. What's for breakfast?" she asked with a smile.

"What do you want?" My arm tightened around her as my hand softly stroked her arm.

"I don't know. Let's go see what we can whip up. Do you know how to cook?" She glanced up at me.

"Yes." I grinned.

"Really? I'm surprised."

"Why?" I chuckled.

"I don't know. I just am."

"I used to help my mom cook all the time. Come on, let's go make some coffee and get breakfast started."

"Can I just say one thing?"

"What?" I smiled.

"I'm happy you can cook because I can't. I can't even boil water." She laughed. "If you said you couldn't cook, we'd be screwed."

"Then I will teach you." I winked as I kissed her soft lips. "And after breakfast, I promise you will be screwed."

As she lifted herself up from me, she grabbed the pillow and hit me with it.

"You're dirty." She grinned.

"You have no idea how dirty I can be, Miss Bell."

After breakfast and a long lovemaking session in the shower, I got dressed and ran to the office to grab some files I wanted to look over before Monday. When I entered the building, I saw Jillian's father in the lobby.

"Mr. Bell? What are you doing here?"

"Please, call me Donald." He held out his hand.

"How did you know that I'd be here today?"

"This is your company, right?"

"Yes."

"People like us are always in the office on Saturdays. I need to talk to you for a moment."

"Sure. Come up to my office. We can talk there."

Taking the elevator up to the twelfth floor, we entered my office and I told him to take a seat.

"What's this about? I'm not really sure I should be talking to you."

"I understand, but you're the only connection I have to Jillian right now. I need you to get her to see me. I need to talk to her alone."

"What about your wife?" I asked as I leaned back in my chair.

"Screw her. She's to blame for all of this and I won't let her stand in the way of me and my daughters anymore. I need to apologize to Jillian and I need to meet Kristen."

"I don't know what you want me to do. I'm pretty positive Jillian won't see you."

"Then it's up to you to make sure she does. Here's my number. Please, Drew. I need your help."

"You don't even know me. How could you trust me?"

"I know enough. I know you're in love with her. I saw it last night and I see it now. People deserve a second chance. Even when they've screwed up so badly, they deserve the chance to make it right. Please, Drew."

I sighed. "I'll talk to her, but I can't guarantee anything."

"I know. I just ask that you please try to convince her."

"We're going to my parents' house for dinner later, so I'll talk to her after. Maybe the two of you can meet up tomorrow."

"Thank you, Drew." He stood up and held out his hand. "You're a good man with a good heart. I can tell that much and Jillian is lucky to have you in her life."

After he walked out of my office, I grabbed the files I needed and headed back to the townhouse. Jillian was going to be upset when I told her that her father paid me a visit, but that conversation would have to wait until tonight.

Chapter Thirty-Three
Jillian

Drew took hold of my hand as we walked up the driveway of his parents' house. As we stepped through the door, he called out to them.

"We're in the kitchen, honey," his mom spoke.

When we walked into the kitchen, his mom was at the island patting together hamburger meat. When I looked at her and she saw me, we stared at each other for a brief moment.

"Jillian?" She smiled.

"Andrea?"

Drew raised his brow as he looked at both of us.

"You two know each other?" he asked.

Andrea washed her hands, walked over to me, and gave me a hug.

"I can't believe this. How are you, honey?"

"I'm good. Oh my God, I can't believe this."

"Wait a minute. You never answered my question. How the hell do you two know each other?"

"I met Jillian at the hospital when she was there with her sister. We had a nice little chat and a bagel and coffee together in the cafeteria."

"Wow. This is unbelievable," Drew spoke.

"Hi there, Jillian. I'm Lou, Drew's dad."

"Hi, Lou. It's nice to meet you."

"Likewise." He grinned.

"Lou, take Drew outside and start the grill. Jillian and I have some catching up to do." Andrea winked.

Drew let go of my hand and stared at me with a confused look on his face as he followed his dad outside.

"Was my son the man you were talking about that day in the hospital?" She smiled.

I looked down in embarrassment. "Yes."

"You two met in Hawaii?" she asked as she continued making the hamburger patties.

"We actually met on the plane to Hawaii. His seat was next to mine and then we ended up at the same hotel."

"I take it you met Jess, then?"

"Oh yeah. I met her and had dinner with them one night."

"She's a real peach. Isn't she?" She smirked.

"She sure is. I ran into her while Kristen and I were having lunch the other day. She was shocked to see me here in New York."

"Oh, I'm sure she was. You said that you didn't know where the man you met lived. How did you and Drew reconnect?"

"We bumped into each other on the street. Like literally bumped into each other."

She gave me a wide grin. "Does Jess know the two of you are seeing each other?"

Before I could answer, Drew and his dad walked in the kitchen and his dad took the plate of burgers out to the grill while Drew stayed behind.

"Oh my gosh. I'm so rude. I hope you like burgers, Jillian. If you don't, I can fix you something else."

"Trust me, Mom. She likes burgers." He grinned.

I narrowed my eye at him and gave his shoulder a nudge. After we finished dinner, Andrea told me and Drew to go sit outside while she and Lou cleaned up. I insisted on helping, but she shoved us out the patio door. Drew handed me a glass of wine and we took a seat on the benches in the gazebo that sat in the center of the yard.

"I can't believe you met my mom at the hospital."

"I can't believe she's your mom. How weird is that?"

"Very weird. In fact, everything in relation to us is weird," he spoke.

"How do you mean?"

"Well, my flight was cancelled and I was put on another flight in the seat next to you. Out of all the hotels in Hawaii, we ended up at the same one. We got to know each other better unexpectedly." He winked. "Then you moved to New York, where I live, which you didn't know, you rented the apartment that I own, which you didn't know, and of all the nurses at the hospital, you happen to have coffee and a bagel with the one who happens to be my mother. And, lastly, of the millions of people in New York City, we run into each other on the street. If you ask me, we were supposed to meet. If we didn't meet on that plane, we would have somewhere else."

"You think?" I bit down on my bottom lip.

"Yeah, and trust me, I'm not a believer in those types of things, but what happened with us made me think twice." He smiled as he grabbed my hand.

A feeling hit the pit of my stomach. It was a feeling of fear, uncertainty. He referred to this as "us." Was I taking it in the wrong context? He was talking about the universe and the grand plan of Cupid. He wasn't a believer and now he was. I feared he wanted a relationship where it was just the two of us. The kind of relationship where we went on dates, had sex, and spent every second we could together.

Then it hit me. That was exactly what was happening with us. He was the first person I met from the escape of my old life. I attached myself to him because he was familiar, not thinking of the repercussions of my behavior. I needed someone because of everything I was going through. A shoulder to cry on. Sex to fill the void that was hiding in the shadows of my life. And now, he wanted more, or he believed it was more than what it really was. Maybe I was just overacting, being paranoid. But the smile on his face alluded to the fact that he considered me his girlfriend.

I'd fallen for him. There was no doubt about that. But I took it too far, being readily available when he asked. My self-journey. What a joke. Did I use Drew to comfort myself when my pity party was in full force? I had never been truly alone. I went from my parents and Grant straight into the arms of Drew Westbrook. My plan was so off course that, once again, I felt lost and confused. I was to create a home base here, spend some time with Kristen, and then jet off to continue my self-journey. But now, I felt more lost than when I left Seattle.

It was getting late, so we said goodbye to his parents and climbed into the Bentley.

"There's something I need to talk to you about, so can we go back to your place?" he spoke.

Nerves flooded my body because I feared he was talking about our relationship.

"Okay."

Walking into my apartment, I threw my keys on the counter and grabbed a bottle of opened wine from the refrigerator.

"What did you want to talk to me about?" I nervously asked as my shaking hands poured some wine into two glasses.

He took in a deep breath. This was it. The moment of truth when he would ask me about our relationship.

"Your father paid me a visit today at the office."

I let out the deep breath I had been holding for what seemed like forever. "My father? Why?"

"He wants to talk to you and he asked for my help."

"I have nothing to say to him or my mother," I spoke as I brought the glass up to my lips.

"It has nothing to do with her. It's just him. I get the feeling he wants to apologize."

"Little too late for that." I softly laughed.

"Just meet with him, Jillian. Hear him out and then move on."

"You were there last night." I raised my voice. "You heard him say how I embarrassed the family and cost him a million dollars and," I shrugged, "I already heard him out and I have moved on."

"I know. But you didn't see him at my office today. He was apologetic and he was begging me for my help. He said that your mother was to blame for all this and that she wasn't going to stand in the way of him and his daughters anymore."

"He played his part. Trust me. He did nothing to stop her and he went along with everything she said and did."

"He screwed up, Jill. Even people who screw up so badly deserve a second chance."

I cocked my head and narrowed my eyes at him. "Are you defending him?"

"No. I'm just saying that you should let him apologize to you. What you do with that apology is up to you. But hear the man out."

"Who are you to tell me what to do? This is my family and it's none of your business," I shouted.

"You made it my business!" He pointed his finger to the floor.

Anger tore up inside me. How dare he.

"Well, I'm making it your un-business. I spent my entire life listening to what other people told me I had to do and I won't stand here and listen to it from some guy that I've only known a few weeks."

"Is that all I am to you? Some guy you've only known a few weeks?"

Shit.

"You're my friend, Drew, and I appreciate everything you've done for me, but this is my life and what goes is what I say. Not what anyone else says."

"I'm your friend, eh?" His voice lowered as he placed his hands in his pants pockets.

"Of course. What else would you be?"

"Nothing. I'm going to go. Do what you think is best for you in regard to your father. I'll see you around, Jillian," he spoke as he walked towards the door.

"Drew, I'm sorry. I need you to understand. My life is seriously complicated right now."

Placing his hand on the doorknob, he lowered his head.

"I do understand."

Chapter Thirty-Four
Drew

In an instant, my heart was broken. She obviously didn't feel the same way as I felt about her. I saw the look on her face at my parents' house when I said the word "us." There was fear in her eyes. Did I truly understand? Sort of. As much as I tried to respect her decision about her self-journey, I had hoped that she would change her mind and that I made her life a little less complicated. I was wrong. Maybe I moved too fast. But that couldn't be helped. She had me the minute she stepped onto the plane and sat down next to me. I'd broken up with many women in my life and I'd never felt this kind of pain before. We were perfect together and for each other. She filled a void in my life that I never knew existed. How the fuck was I going to get over her?

The next morning as I was in the kitchen sipping on some coffee and wallowing in self-pity, Jane walked through the door.

"Good morning, Drew." She brightly smiled.

"Hey, Jane." I glanced up at her. "Why are you here? It's your day off."

"I needed to check on some things in the pantry. I'm heading to the grocery store today, so I want to make sure I don't forget anything. What's wrong?"

"Nothing."

"You can't fool me, Drew. I know when something is wrong." She walked over to the coffee pot and poured a cup of coffee.

"I don't want to talk about it."

"Does this have something to do with Jillian?" she asked as she took a seat next to me.

"I'm pretty sure we won't be seeing each other anymore."

"What? Why?"

"Her life is complicated right now, as she says. The day I met her on the plane was her wedding day and she had just left her fiancé at the altar. It's a long story."

"I see. So she's not ready to jump into another relationship yet. That's understandable. Just give her some time, she'll come around. You are a very hard man to resist."

"She's on a self-discovery journey and I've known that. She made it very clear when we first met on the plane. I was trying to be careful and respect that, but I moved too fast. I lost her, Jane."

"Give her some space. Let her discover herself and then she'll come back to you. I know she will. Patience is a virtue, Drew."

"Patience is something I don't have when it comes to her. I feel destroyed inside."

"That's because you love her. Love hurts. You've never truly been in love, so this is new to you. If you love her that much, then you'll let her go. Let her do what she needs to do. Isn't her happiness all you want?"

Taking the last sip of coffee from my cup, I sighed as I looked over at Jane.

"Yes. I just want her to be happy and live the life she wants and deserves."

"Then there you have it." She patted my back. "Sometimes letting go of the things we love is the hardest part of life. But if she was meant to be yours and you were meant to be hers, you'll find your way back to each other. Don't lose yourself in the process, Drew. Stay strong and hold on to that little bit of hope."

"Thanks, Jane."

"You're welcome. I'm off to the grocery store. I'll see you in the morning."

****

Jillian

I was a horrible person. I knew what I said would hurt him. The look of sadness in his eyes stabbed me straight through the heart. A wound that was so deep, I hated myself. I lay in bed, exhausted from all the tears that fell last night. Had I not said what I did, I would be wrapped up in the comfort and safety of Drew's arms. Instead, I was alone. Which was what I wanted, right? Fuck if I knew what I wanted anymore. This wasn't how things were supposed to happen. I was in no position to fall for a man and Kristen wasn't supposed to be dying. My life had changed in the blink of an eye, and now, I found it was too much to handle.

Climbing out of bed, I showered, got myself dressed, and looked at my phone, debating whether or not to call my father. I couldn't stop thinking about what Drew said about everyone deserving a second chance. Was I really that much of a cold-hearted bitch that I couldn't at least let my father apologize to me? My mind went back to the conversation I had with Ano, the one where he told me that I needed to be fearless to continue my journey. Was I scared to let my father apologize to me? The deeper I searched into my soul for answers, the more confused I became. Dialing his number, I took in a deep long breath.

"Hello," he answered.

"Dad, it's Jillian. I was told you wanted to talk."

"Jillian, thank you for calling. I had hoped you would."

"If you want to talk, meet me at The Lake in Central Park at three o'clock."

"I'll be there. Thank you, Jillian."

"See you soon." I hung up before he had a chance to say anything else.

I had two hours before I had to meet my father in Central Park, so I headed to Kristen's and Noah's apartment. I needed to talk to her and warn her of our father's intentions.

"Hey, you." Kristen smiled as I walked through the door.

"Hey." I kissed her cheek. "Are you and Noah busy?"

"We're just going over some wedding stuff. Are you okay?"

"I need to talk to you about something," I spoke as I set my purse down and took a seat on the couch.

"It sounds serious," Noah spoke as he walked into the room.

"I guess you can say it is. There's something I haven't told you yet," I spoke as I looked at Kristen. "Friday night, at the charity event, I ran into my parents."

"Shit. What were they doing there?" Kristen asked.

"Apparently, they were invited. Who knows? The whole night was a clusterfuck with them. Anyway, things were said and there were a lot of raised voices. I told our father about our relationship and I also told him about your illness. He wants to meet you."

"Fuck him!" Noah shouted.

Kristen put her hand up to him. "Noah, please."

"You seriously aren't considering it, are you?" he asked her.

"What harm would it do? I think I should at least meet my father before I die."

I sat there and stared at the brave and beautiful woman who was my sister. She was filled with courage and strength and I admired her greatly for it.

"Are you sure, Kristen? How can you forgive him for what he did?"

A small smile crossed her lips as she reached over and took hold of my hand.

"Forgiveness is what gives us strength in life, Jill. Forgiveness sets you free."

"I'm meeting him in Central Park. Supposedly, he wants to apologize to me."

"What about Patricia?" she asked.

"I'm not so sure things are good between them. Not that they ever were, but he made a comment to Drew that she will no longer stand in the way of him and his daughters."

"Speaking of Drew, how were his parents?"

"You're never going to believe this."

"Now what?" She cocked her head.

"You know your nurse, Andrea?"

"Yeah." She frowned.

"She's his mother."

"No way! So the son she was talking about all that time was Drew?"

"Yes."

"And you connected with her right away and even had coffee and a bagel with her?"

"Yep. I sure did."

"Not knowing that was his mother?"

"Nope. I had no clue." I shook my head.

She let out a long sigh. "The universe is smacking you right upside the head, Jill."

"Yeah. Well, I said something last night that hurt Drew and I'm not sure he'll be coming around anymore."

"Oh for fuck sakes. What did you do?"

"He just can't understand that I can't be with anyone right now."

"Oh, Jill. Drew is the best thing that has ever happened to you."

"I really don't want to talk about it right now. Please understand."

"Okay. But we're going to talk about it soon. Oh, by the way, after the wedding, Noah and I are going on a honeymoon." She beamed with excitement.

"Where to?" I asked.

"Italy. I know it's last minute, but he wasn't sure if he could get the time off work. But his boss gave him two weeks."

"Wow. That's great. I'm so happy for you. But are you well enough to travel?"

"I'll never be well enough again, sis. But I'll be okay. Italy is a place I've always wanted to see and my future husband is going to make sure I get to." She smiled.

I looked at my watch. It was time to leave to go meet my father.

"Just promise me you'll take it easy while you're there." I got up from the couch and gave her a hug.

"You worry too much." She laughed.

Chapter Thirty-Five
Jillian

My stomach was a bundle of nerves as I saw my father sitting down underneath a large tree, out of the sun and away from the crowd of people who were enjoying the warm sunny day. As I slowly walked towards him, I could see the sadness that resided on his face. It was a look that I'd only seen once in my life and that was when my grandmother passed away.

"Hello, Jillian." His lips gave way to a small subtle smile.

"Daddy," I spoke as I sat down next to him.

"How are you?" he asked.

"I'm here. So what did you want to talk about?" I asked as I stared straight ahead, not being able to look him in the eyes.

"I want to apologize to you for the other night. After giving our discussion some serious thought, I now understand why you did it. Why you left us and Grant."

Looking down and fidgeting with my hands, I spoke, "You do?"

"Yeah, sweetheart, I do. I need you to understand that your mother and I only wanted what was best for you. We wanted you to be a successful, well-educated adult. Unfortunately, we went about it the wrong way and I'm sorry."

"You wanted me to be the perfect child. The daughter you and Mom could show off and boast about to all your high society friends. You never gave me the chance to be the person I wanted to be."

"And who do you want to be?"

"I want to be me. You brainwashed me into believing that I had to do and act in such a manner, that if I didn't, I would be nothing but a disappointment and a disgrace to you both. Did you know that I hated ballet? Yet I was forced to take years of lessons because that's what all upper class girls took."

"I thought you loved ballet, Jill."

"No, I hated it. Just like I hated that damn private school you made me go to. I wanted to be like the normal kids and attend a public school. I wanted to meet kids outside of our upper class circle. Kids who weren't given everything they ever wanted and lived in the real world. I wanted to explore what other things life had to offer. Not just what money could buy. And as for law school, I don't even want to be a lawyer, but it was shoved down my throat since I was five years old."

"Why didn't you come to me with all this?"

"I tried, but you were always gone or too busy."

"And your mother?"

"She would tell me to stop being ridiculous and she didn't want to hear any more nonsense out of my mouth. After a while, I gave up and sank into a depression that took me years to get out of."

"You never seemed depressed to me."

"That's because I was good at hiding it. I had no choice but to pretend to be the happy and perfect daughter of Donald and Patricia Bell, when really, I was dying inside."

"And you talked to your grandmother about all of this?"

"Yes. She knew something was wrong with me when I spent the summer at her house when I was fifteen years old. And you want to know how she knew? We were shopping at Saks and I was arrested for shoplifting."

"My god, Jillian. Why?"

"A cry for help. A cry for attention. A cry to do something that nobody would expect of me."

"I'm sorry, baby." He placed his hand gently on my leg.

"I was released and it never went on my record. Grandma knew the judge and had a long talk with him. We talked about everything that summer. She was the only person who understood besides Kellan. That's why she left me the money for when I turned twenty-one. She knew the day would come when I would just walk away."

"I'm so sorry. I had no idea. I don't know what to say, Jillian, except that I was a shit father who cared more about his company than his family. I wasn't there for you and I always sided with your mother when I shouldn't have. Sometimes it was just easier to agree with her."

"I know what you mean."

"Why didn't you leave when you turned twenty-one?"

I sighed. "I was still in college and I had worked too hard to get to where I was just to throw it all away."

"I'm afraid to ask why you waited for your wedding day."

"I think you know the answer to that." I glanced over at him.

He slowly nodded his head. "Revenge."

"Yep." I bit down on my bottom lip.

"You had it planned all along."

"Yep."

He sighed. "I want to make things right with you, Jillian. I know there aren't enough apologies in the world, but please know that I am truly sorry. As for your sister, doing what I did to her and her mother was one of my biggest regrets. I thought about her often and I even saw her once while I was here in New York on business. She was having dinner with her mother one night at a restaurant I was at. They didn't see me, but I sure saw them and I stared at my daughter for as long as they were there. I wanted to reach out to her, but I couldn't. I was too afraid."

"Why did you do it, Dad? Why did you just leave her like that?"

"Because I didn't have a choice. Your mother threatened to divorce me and take everything I had worked so hard for my entire life. If it got out that I had a child by another woman, it would have been disastrous both personally and professionally. You have to understand that, Jill."

"I will never understand a parent never acknowledging his child."

There was a moment of silence between us as I stared straight ahead at the people who surrounded the area. The laughter of children filled the air, couples sitting on their blankets enjoying a picnic, and friends just hanging out enjoying the beautiful day.

"I want to meet her, Jill. I need to meet my daughter."

I swallowed hard, finding it difficult to say the words. "I'll set it up."

"Thank you. You have no idea how much it means to me to hear you say that."

"Where's Mom?" I asked.

"She flew back to Seattle this morning. I told her that I had some business to attend to while I was here. Things aren't good with us."

Bringing my knees to my chest, I spoke, "They never were."

My father placed his hand on my knee and I turned my head and looked at him. What I saw was a broken man. A man who didn't know what to do anymore. A man who looked lost and was desperately trying to find his way back home. The words Kristen said to me kept replaying over and over in my head. "Forgiveness gives you strength and forgiveness will set you free." Forgiveness was something I shouldn't have feared and it was time to let that fear go. If I was going to continue to find myself, I had no choice. Ano was right; I needed to face and come to terms with what I had done and it started with my father.

"I forgive you, Dad." I laid my head on his shoulder.

He leaned his head on mine. "Thank you, Jill. You are and will always be my little girl. No matter where life takes you, I'll always love you."

Chapter Thirty-Six
Drew

I drove to the Hamptons and rented a boat for the day. This was something I wanted to do with Jillian and had planned on asking her, but in light of the current circumstances, I went alone. My heart ached and I thought about her every second. I was more than broken-hearted. I was pissed. Pissed at myself for moving too fast and pissed at her for not seeing that I could be a part of her self-journey.

As I sailed across the ocean, taking in the warmth of the breeze that swept across my face, I reflected on my life. Maybe this was karma for leaving Marley at the altar all those years ago. Maybe it was payback for all the women who wanted more from me that I cut loose and left broken. I'd never been hurt before, and now, I felt what all those women had felt. I'd finally found true love, even though I wasn't looking for it, and she made it clear that she didn't feel the same way. This was definitely karma biting me in the ass ten times over for my past behavior with women. How the fuck was I going to get over her? I didn't know how because I never had to before. She consumed me and the need to be with her was too strong for me to move on. I didn't want to move on. I'd never find someone like Jillian again. She was my one chance and now, my chance was gone.

As I pulled in and docked the boat, I heard someone calling my name.

"Drew!" Liam shouted from a couple boats over.

Turning around, I saw him, Avery, Oliver, and Delilah waving at me.

"Hey." I nodded as I walked over to him and Oliver and we shook hands.

"What are you doing here, bro?" Liam asked.

"I decided to go out on the boat for a while. Hi, Avery, Delilah." I gave them each a hug.

"Hi, Drew. It's good to see you."

Looking over my shoulder, Liam spoke, "Where's Jillian?"

The look on my face must have said it all because, instantly, the smile that was on Liam's face quickly dissipated.

"She didn't come."

"Hey, Avery and Delilah want to go shopping, so why don't you, me, and Oliver go hit up a bar for a couple of drinks and maybe some burgers," Liam spoke.

"Sounds like a plan to me." Oliver grinned.

Did I really want company right now? No, because they knew something was wrong and I'd be forced to talk about Jillian with them. Hell, maybe talking about her with someone would make me feel a little better.

"Sure. Sounds good."

****

The three of us took a seat at a table out on the patio of a place called Surf. As soon as our waitress brought over our drinks, the questions started rolling in.

"So what happened?" Liam asked.

"With?" I took a sip of my scotch.

"Jillian?" His brow arched.

I took in a sharp breath. "She doesn't feel the same way about me as I do her."

"Are you sure about that?" Oliver asked.

"Bullshit!" Liam exclaimed as he sipped on his drink. "I've seen the two of you together and I know the look."

"The look?"

"The one that says 'I'm so into him.'" Liam grinned.

"What?" Oliver asked as he cocked his head at his brother. "Are you some kind of woman expert now?"

"I always have been, dear brother. It's the same look Delilah always has with you and it's the look that Avery gets when she's with me." He winked.

Oliver rolled his eyes. "Drew, did she tell you that she didn't feel the same way?"

"She told me I was her friend and nothing more." I finished off my scotch.

Just as I said that, the waitress walked over and set down our food.

"Hey, let me ask you something," Liam said to her.

"Sure." She smiled brightly at him.

"There's a look women get when they're really into a guy, right?"

"I suppose so," she answered. "I mean, I don't know for me, but I've seen a look on my girlfriends' faces when they're really into someone."

"Describe that look." Liam smiled.

"Liam!" Oliver voiced.

"Quiet, Oliver." Liam waved his hand. "Go on." He smiled at the waitress.

"I don't know. It's like a twinkle in their eye or just an overall sweetness that sweeps over their face. It's hard to describe. Kind of like a glow."

"Exactly!" Liam pointed his finger at her. "Thank you for your help. I will make sure to compensate you with a generous tip." He winked.

She gave us each a smile and casually walked away after we ordered another round of drinks.

"See. I saw that glow or twinkle with Jillian."

Oliver rolled his eyes and I couldn't help but chuckle.

"Go ahead and don't believe, Oliver, but it's true. And you, my bro friend," he pointed at me, "need to claim what is yours."

"And how do I do that? She doesn't want a relationship. She's very adamant about that."

Liam waved his hand in front of his face. "So was Avery and look at us now."

"Excuse me," Oliver spoke. "If I remember correctly, she was the one who went after you in California."

"Details. Details, Oliver. The point is she realized how much she loved me. So, here's the plan, Drew. Get in touch with her and tell her that you gave it some serious thought and friends is what is best for the both of you. Make the agreement on her terms. Women love a good fight and when they realize we men aren't fighting for them anymore, that's when it hits them."

"Is that so?" Oliver cocked his head.

"Well, not in your case. But you were pretty fucked up."

Again, I let out a chuckle.

"Listen, Drew," Oliver spoke. "If you love Jillian that much, then you have to go after her."

"No. No. No." Liam shook his head. "This is totally different. Delilah loved you and you pushed her away. Jillian knows she loves Drew but is too afraid to admit it because she's trying to find herself. She's scared that if she confesses her feelings, she'll be deterred from her journey."

"So you're a shrink now?" Oliver asked.

"I should be, right?" Liam winked. "Anyway, Drew, back to what I was saying. You need to call her bluff. Be friends and then, when the time is right, make her jealous. Go out with someone and make sure Jillian sees you with her. If anything, seeing the man you care about with someone else always sparks a little bit of jealousy. Maybe then, she'll realize what she let go."

"Were you a woman in a past life or something?" Oliver asked him.

"Maybe." He frowned as he placed his hand on his chin.

It was getting late and I had to drive back to the city.

"Thanks for the food and advice, guys, but I'm going to head back now."

As I was driving back to the city, I couldn't stop thinking about Liam's advice. It actually sounded like a good plan. Being friends with Jillian was better than being nothing with her at all. Tomorrow, I'd text her and put my plan into motion.

****

After I returned from a meeting, I pulled my phone from my pocket and took in a deep breath as I typed Jillian a text message. Fuck it. This needed to be done over the phone, so I called her.

"Hello," she answered.

"Hi, it's Drew."

"Hi, Drew." Her voice was unsure.

"I just wanted to tell you that I'm sorry about the other night. I didn't mean to walk out like I did and I want you to know that I fully understand."

"It's okay. I understand why you left."

"Listen, Jillian. We're friends and I don't want that to end."

"I don't either, Drew."

"Good. I also want you to know that I'll always be here for you if you need someone to talk to, whether it be about your parents, Kristen, or anything about yourself. I'm just a phone call away."

"Thank you. I appreciate it. I really do and it means a lot to me to hear you say that."

"You're welcome. I have to hang up now. I have a meeting to get to."

"Okay. We'll talk soon. Bye, Drew."

"Bye, Jillian."

I let out a deep breath as I hit the end button on my phone.

Chapter Thirty-Seven
Jillian

I set my phone down and looked at Kristen, who was sitting across from me.

"Well? What did he want?" she asked.

"He said he wants us to be friends."

"Good man. Is that what you want?"

"Yes. Of course."

"Well, then you can't sleep with him. Because you can't have a friends-with-benefits type of relationship."

"I know. He told me to call him if I ever need anything."

"Is he coming to the wedding?" She bit down on her bottom lip. "Because I just assumed he was."

"I don't know. Did you invite him?"

"I thought you already did." She frowned.

"We never really talked about it."

Rolling her eyes, she sighed. "Give me his number. I'll ask him. After all, he is the one who got us that wonderful room. He should be there."

"I agree," I spoke and then rattled off his number to her.

Drew calling me and wanting to still be friends meant a lot to me. Maybe someday, once I discovered who I was, we could be more. But for now, friends were what we had to remain, even though I missed him like crazy. I couldn't use him to fulfill my own needs. It wasn't fair to him. Truly loving someone before you love yourself wasn't an option. No exceptions.

"He said he'd love to come." Kristen grinned.

A small smile crossed my lips. "Good. I'm happy he can make it."

****

Kristen and my father met later that night. Noah wasn't thrilled, but he put on a happy face for Kristen because this was what she wanted. I stood there and watched my father cry as he hugged her and the two of them sat down on the couch and talked for a few hours. It made me wonder that if Kristen wasn't dying, would she have wanted to meet him.

"I have to ask you a question and I don't want you to get mad at me," I spoke.

"What?"

"If you weren't dying, would you have wanted to meet Dad?"

"Yes. I still would have wanted to meet him."

"Why?" I asked in confusion.

"Because I'm strong enough to know that people make mistakes. There's not one person on the face of this Earth that hasn't made a mistake or two in their life. It's not healthy to hold grudges and my mother always taught me that. Believe it or not, she forgave him a long time ago."

"Really?"

"Yes. I wish you could have met her. She was the most beautiful person you'd ever meet. She was so full of wisdom and knowledge."

"No wonder Dad stayed with her for over a year."

"She told me that she couldn't hate him because he gave her the most precious gift anyone could ever give someone: me."

Tears started to fill my eyes. "Didn't she ever meet anyone else?"

"She dated a lot. But she said no one could ever fill the shoes that were Dad's."

I reached over and placed my hand on hers as we both sat there and let the tears fall freely down our cheeks.

****

Drew

Being invited to Kristen and Noah's wedding thrilled me because then I would get to see Jillian again. Remembering what Liam had said, I called Lia into my office.

"Yes, Drew." She smiled as she walked in.

"Have a seat. There's something I would like to ask you."

"What is it?"

"I don't know how to ask you this without sounding like a complete dick."

She laughed. "Just come out with it."

"Would you attend a wedding with me on Saturday evening at the Harmonie Club?"

"Is Jillian going to be there?"

Clearing my throat, I spoke, "Yes. She'll be there."

"She hasn't met me yet. So if we walk in together, she may think we're seeing each other." Her eye narrowed at me.

"Perhaps." I folded my hands. "It's a dick move, I know. You can thank Liam for that."

She laughed. "I get it. I really do. And yes, I will attend the wedding with you."

"Really? You don't think I'm an asshole for doing this?"

"No. I don't think that at all."

"Thanks, Lia. Go buy yourself a new dress on me. Put it on the business account and Liam will babysit Gretchen and Gigi for you." I smiled.

"Really? That's great because my babysitter is out of town this week and won't be back until Monday."

"Consider it done."

"The girls will be excited. They like Liam and Avery."

I gave her a smile as she walked out of my office. Picking up my phone, I dialed Liam.

"What's up, bro?" he answered.

"Lia is going with me to Jillian's sister's wedding on Saturday night and you're babysitting Gretchen and Gigi for her."

"Dude, I have tickets to the playoffs for that night and Avery is going out with her girlfriends."

"Looks like you're going to have to watch the game from home. Your idea, man. Your idea."

He sighed. "Fine. I just didn't think you'd do it so soon. I'll have Sophie come over so she can keep the girls entertained and I can watch the game. Man, you really suck right now."

I let out a laugh. "Thanks, Liam. I'll talk to you soon."

****

Jillian

Cupping my hands over my mouth, tears filled my eyes as I stood and stared at my sister in her wedding dress.

"Stop it. I'm warning you." Kristen pointed at me.

"You look so beautiful. Oh my God, wait until Noah sees you."

"You're not going to disappear, are you?" She grinned.

I laughed. "No. I'm not going anywhere."

The door opened and my father walked in. Walking over, he kissed my cheek. "You look beautiful, Jillian."

"Thanks, Daddy." I smiled.

Reaching over and taking hold of Kristen's hands, he spoke in a low voice.

"Are you ready, sweetheart?"

"Yeah, Dad. I'm more than ready."

Kristen had asked our father the night they met if he would do the honor of walking her down the aisle on her wedding day. He was in shock and it took him a few seconds before he could answer her. He never left New York and told my mother that he was tied up on emergency business and that he'd be flying back home on Sunday. She asked him if he had spent time with me and he was truthful and said yes. He also told her that he met Kristen. My mother wasn't happy about that. If anyone needed to go in search of themselves, it was her. Things between the two of us still weren't settled and I wasn't sure if they'd ever be.

The music started to play and I took my place to walk down the aisle first. Glancing at the guests as I slowly walked to the music, I spotted Drew sitting next to a woman. Perhaps she was one of Kristen's friends. Yeah. That was who she was; she was a friend of my sister. I wasn't giving it a second thought because there was no way he'd bring someone to her wedding.

Tears fell as I watched Kristen and Noah exchange vows, and you could hear the sniffles of the guests throughout the room. As happy as I was for them, it broke my heart. Once the ceremony was over and the guests were leaving the room to go up to the reception, I saw Drew and the woman he was sitting next to get up, and he placed his hand on the small of her back. A sick feeling erupted in the pit of my stomach. He did bring someone with him. What the fuck!

"What's wrong?" Kellan asked as he walked over to me.

"Nothing. Why?"

"You look really upset all of a sudden."

"Who me?" I pointed to myself. "I'm not upset at all. Now come on, we have some celebrating to do." I smiled.

"You can't fool me, Bean. I know you all too well." He hooked his arm around me.

Chapter Thirty-Eight
Jillian

I wasn't going to give it another thought. Nope. Not one. This was Kristen and Noah's big day and my focus had to be on them. While the two of them walked around greeting their guests, Kellan and I went over to the bar for a much-needed drink. Just as the bartender handed me a glass of champagne, I turned around to see Drew and the girl he brought standing in front of me.

"Hi, Jillian." He smiled.

"Hi, Drew."

"I would like you to meet Lia. Lia, this is my friend, Jillian."

"It's so nice to meet you." She smiled as she held out her slender hand.

"Nice to meet you too, Lia." I flashed my perfected smile.

"Nice to finally meet you in person, Kellan." Drew grinned as they shook hands.

"Good to meet you too."

"I see your father is here," Drew spoke as he placed his hand in his pocket and held a glass of scotch with the other.

"Yes. We had a long talk and Kristen asked him to be here tonight."

"Good. I'm happy to hear that you two worked things out. What about your mother?"

"Nah. She's back in Seattle. I haven't heard from her. Which is okay."

"Well, we're going to head back to our table. Talk to you later?"

"Yeah. Sure. Enjoy the wedding." I smiled.

I couldn't even begin to tell you the feeling that washed over me. It was a mixture of different emotions. Sadness, anger, surprise, shock, just to name a few.

"You can't be mad or upset, Bean," Kellan spoke. "You did tell him that he's only a friend."

"I know that, Kel, and I'm not upset."

He rolled his eyes. "Have you forgotten that you can't hide anything from me?" He kissed the side of my head.

"Hey, sweetheart. What's going on with you and Drew? I see he's here with someone," my dad asked.

"Drew and I are just friends, Daddy. Nothing more."

Confusion set in as he looked at me. "I thought you two were dating."

I swallowed hard. "No. We're just friends."

"Jillian, what's—"

"Come on, Dad. They want everyone to sit down for dinner."

Taking my seat next to Kristen at the bridal table, I couldn't help but glance over at Drew and Lia, taking notice of how the two of them were talking and laughing. For someone who wanted more than just friendship, it didn't take him too long to move on to someone else. Was I really surprised? Not a bit. Look at how fast he moved from Jess to me. Fucking douchebag.

"I know that look and I know right now you're angry," Kristen spoke in my ear. "But you can't be and you have no right to be. You made it very—"

Putting my hand up, I interrupted her. "I know. I made it very clear that we're only friends."

After we ate, it was time for Kristen and Noah to take their first dance as husband and wife. Kellan walked over and hooked his arm around me.

"Your dad apologized to me."

"He did?"

"Yep. You know I never had anything against him. But Patricia." He shuddered and I couldn't help but laugh.

After their dance ended, it was an open floor for all the guests to dance the night away. The song "All of Me" by John Legend started to play. Kristen and my dad were the first on the dance floor while other couples followed behind.

"Come on, Jilly, let's dance." Kellan smiled as he led me to the dance floor.

As we were dancing, I looked over to see Drew and Lia on the dance floor. My heart started to rapidly beat and I buried my face into Kellan's shoulder.

"It's okay," he whispered.

"I'm not sure it is."

Just as the song ended, the DJ announced to switch partners with the couple dancing next to us as he played "Stay with Me" by Sam Smith.

"Oh hello, darling." Kellan smiled as he took Lia's hand.

Shit. Shit. Shit, I thought to myself as I took in a deep breath and placed my hand in Drew's.

"We've never danced together," he spoke.

"No. We haven't."

His hand wrapped around my waist felt good as did our hands that were locked together. His lips were inches from my ear. I could feel myself trembling.

"I like this song," he whispered in my ear. "I don't want you to leave will you hold my hand," were the next words whispered.

I tightened and I knew he'd felt it.

"Relax, Jillian," he spoke as he continued singing in my ear. "Oh won't you stay with me, 'cause you're all I need."

"I am relaxed."

"But, darling, stay with me."

On that note, the song ended and I couldn't get away from Drew fast enough.

"Thanks for the dance." He smiled as he turned to Lia and they both headed back to their table.

I couldn't breathe. Something was wrong and I needed air. Kellan sensed it, so he grabbed my hand and led me outside on the balcony for some fresh air.

"I can't breathe, Kel. I feel like I'm going to pass out."

He gripped my shoulders tight.

"Look at me. Calm down. Take in a slow deep breath. Come on, Jill. You can do it. Slow, deep breath." He stared into my eyes.

Suddenly, my heart started to calm itself and my breathing returned to normal.

"Good girl." He gave a small smile. "You, my darling, just had a panic attack."

"It's just everything that's going on."

"You mean it's Drew. You were fine until you danced with him."

I smacked him on the chest. "Why the hell would you let me dance with him?"

"Ouch. Because he and Lia were the couple standing next to us and he's your friend. Just like us. You didn't freak out when we danced."

"And you didn't sing to me either!"

"Oh." His lips formed the letter. "He sang in your ear? How romantic, Jilly."

"Ugh! He's with someone. What an asshole."

"Did you ever stop to think that maybe that woman he's with is just a friend?"

"No! You can't just be friends with Drew Westbrook."

"Come here." He wrapped his arms around me and pulled me into him. "We need to go back inside before people come looking for us. You can feel sorry for yourself in the morning, but tonight, you need to stay strong for Kristen."

"You're right." I broke our embrace. "And I'm not feeling sorry for myself. I need a drink," I spoke as I walked back inside.

As I headed over to the bar, Drew followed me.

"Are you okay, Jillian? I saw you and Kellan outside."

"Yeah. I'm great. I just needed some fresh air. It's a little warm in here."

"It is warm."

"Lia seems really nice," I spoke as the bartender handed me a glass of wine.

"She is. She's really sweet."

Sting. Burn. Stab.

"Kristen and Noah are leaving tomorrow for Italy," I spoke out of nowhere.

"Good for them. Italy is beautiful. I love it there."

"I've never been." I sipped my wine. Okay, I gulped down my wine.

"You should try to get there someday. I think you'd love it there."

"Maybe I'll head there on my next adventure."

"Let me know what you think," he spoke.

"I will."

"I think Lia and I are going to head out. Her kids are with the babysitter and she needs to get home."

Kids? Was he serious?

"She has kids?"

"Yeah. Two beautiful little girls."

"That's nice." I gave my perfected smile.

"Have a good night, Jillian."

I gulped. "You too, Drew. Thanks for coming."

"It was my pleasure. Oh, and by the way, the bill is already taken care of. My gift to the bride and groom."

"Drew, you didn't have to do that."

"I know. I wanted to." He winked as he walked away.

Chapter Thirty-Nine
Drew

As soon as Lia and I climbed into the Bentley, I looked over at her.

"I feel like a total dick for doing this."

"Don't, Drew. She was upset I was there with you. She kept staring at us all night."

"You think?"

"I know. I'm a woman. I can read other women. She was definitely not happy."

I sighed.

We pulled up to Liam's townhouse so she could get the girls and then Roland was going to drive her home. Upon walking into Liam's house, the girls came running and gave Lia a hug.

"Where's Uncle Liam?" I asked them.

"In the family room." They giggled.

Walking into the room, I saw Sophie standing in front of Liam with what looked like makeup brushes.

"What's going on in here?" I smiled.

Laughter ripped out of me when Liam turned around and his face was all painted with makeup.

"Shut up, Drew."

"But you look so pretty."

"Ha ha, very funny. Little smarty pants Sophie over here made me sign a piece a paper that I would let her put makeup on me if she let me watch the playoff game."

Pulling my phone from my pocket, I quickly snapped his picture.

"Damn you, Drew!" he yelled.

"Sorry, bro, or should I say sis? It was too good of an opportunity to pass up." I laughed.

"How did it go with Jill?"

Staring at him, I couldn't seem to hold a conversation while he was wearing all that makeup. The bright red lipstick was really bugging me.

"You need to take that makeup off, dude. I just can't talk to you like that."

He rolled his eyes. "Soph, go get the face wipes."

"Okay, Uncle Liam." She giggled.

Sophie returned with the face wipes and Liam started to wipe off the makeup.

"Okay. Go on. I want details."

"Lia said she could tell Jillian was upset."

"Okay. That's good."

"Not really. I didn't want to upset her and I'm sure I made matters worse when we danced together and I sang in her ear."

"Nice one, Drew." He smiled.

"Then why do I feel like a complete dick?"

"Listen, bro. You did what you had to do. I mean, sometimes we have to hurt the people we love in order for them to wake up. Trust me, she'll be back in your life soon."

"And if she isn't?"

He stopped wiping his face and looked at me with confusion.

"Well, I don't know. Then maybe I was wrong about her, but I doubt it. Have a little faith."

"I'm going to head home. Thanks again for watching the girls. Are you taking Sophie home?"

"Nah, she's spending the night. But no more makeup!" He pointed at her and she giggled.

I chuckled as I headed to the door.

"Good night, Miss Sophie."

"Good night, Mr. Drew. Be careful walking home."

"Yeah, try not to trip over any bushes," Liam yelled.

After stripping out of my suit, I put on my pajama bottoms, poured myself a drink, and climbed into bed. *Now what?* I thought to myself. Seeing her in that long strapless plum-colored dress with her hair pinned up in curls really did me in. The minute she walked down that aisle, I was even more captivated than the first time I had ever laid eyes on her. I never knew that I needed stability. I mean, I did have some stability in my life with my company, but I needed more in my life. A woman who would stand by my side that I could hold and take care of. That was what I never realized I needed until I met Jillian. She was all the stability I needed.

****

Jillian

My aching fucking head. Shit. I drank way too much last night. The struggle was real trying to get out bed. When I finally managed it, I stumbled into the kitchen, where I found Kellan leaning over the counter, drinking his coffee.

"Morning, Miss Hangover." He smiled.

"Shut up," I growled.

"Be nice or you won't get any coffee." He poured some into a cup and handed it to me.

"Ugh. Why did you let me drink so much?" I laid my head down on the counter.

"If you recall, I tried to stop you, but you weren't hearing it."

"What time does your flight leave?"

"In about four hours. So sober up."

"I don't want you to leave." I pouted as I looked up at him.

"I don't want to go either. I miss you, Bean. Maybe I'll move here. I can get a job anywhere."

"Don't toy with me, Kel."

"Seriously, Jill. I'm being serious. I'm over Seattle."

"What about your parents?"

He smiled. "What about yours?"

"Good point."

"I'm sure there's a company on Wall Street that would hire me with my financial background. I'm going to start looking as soon as I get back to Seattle."

"I would love for you to move here." I wrapped my arms around him.

"You stink like alcohol. Go take a shower." He kissed the top of my head.

As the hot water streamed down me, the first thing that came to my mind was Drew. I vaguely remembered having a dream about him last night. We were in Hawaii on the beach and the sun had just set. I sank down on the shower floor and brought my knees up, hugging them tight as the water beat down on me. I was fighting with myself. Fighting to detach myself from the man I was in love with. But the fight in me was quickly leaving, and the strength I thought I had, wasn't there anymore. All I kept picturing in my head was him and Lia and wondering if they had sex after she put her kids to bed. The thought of him with another woman made me sick. I blew it. He'd moved on because I was too selfish and only thought of myself. He'd given up on me. Just like I had given up on myself all those years ago.

After managing to finish my shower, I got dressed, and Kellan and I headed to the airport.

"Call me as soon as you land." I hugged him goodbye.

"I will, Bean. Do me a favor."

"What?"

"Hurry up and find yourself so you can be happy. I hate to say this because you know how much I love you, but I think this whole self-journey thing is destroying you. You're a beautiful, intelligent, and independent woman, and it's okay to fall in love with someone. When we'd talk while Drew was around, you were the happiest I'd ever seen you. I don't want to sit back and watch you walk on the path of destruction again. Been there, done that, and I won't let you do it again. You can find out who you are and loving someone isn't going to change that."

"Don't you have a plane to catch?" I wiped the tear that formed in my eye.

He kissed my forehead. "I love you. Make some good decisions." He winked.

"I love you too. Don't forget to call me."

"Who would ever forget to call you?" He smiled.

Chapter Forty
Drew

I needed to come clean about Lia to Jillian. Why the fuck did I listen to Liam? As I pulled out my phone, a text message from her came through.

"Hey. Can we talk?"

"Of course. When?"

"In about an hour. I have to say goodbye to my dad first."

"Where at?"

"My place?"

"I'll see you in an hour."

Seeing her text made me smile, yet I was nervous as to what she wanted to talk about. Maybe it was about us, or maybe it was about Lia. Either way, I was telling her the truth and I hoped she didn't hate me for it.

****

Jillian

"There's something I want to talk to you about," my dad spoke as I took a seat on the couch in his suite.

"What is it?"

"I don't want to make your life more complicated than it already is, but I feel you have the right to know."

"Okay."

"When I get back to Seattle, I'm telling your mother that I'm filing for divorce."

I wasn't shocked in the least. In fact, I felt they should have divorced years ago. Kids never want to see their parents get divorced, but in my case, I sort of welcomed it.

"I understand, Dad."

"I lost the woman who I believed was the love of my life twenty-four years ago and I'm not about to live in a loveless unhappy marriage anymore. If there's one thing you taught me, Jill, it's that you don't have to settle for anything in life." He placed his hand on my cheek.

"What about everything you worked so hard for? Mom will try to take you for everything you have."

"I know, but she won't get everything." He gave a small smile. "That's not for you to worry about. I'll be fine."

"And what about Kristen? What happened all those years ago will get out."

"And I'll be the one telling it. Listen, I have to go now, sweetheart." We both got up from the couch and I wrapped my arms around him, hugging him tight. "I like Drew, Jill. I think he's a good man and I know he loves you. Don't do what I did all those years ago. Don't be afraid and just let life lead you in the right direction. It led you to Drew for a reason. I love you and I just want you to be happy."

"I know, Dad. I love you too."

"Goodbye, sweet girl." He kissed my forehead. "Stay in touch with your old man."

"I will."

I gave him one last hug before he climbed into the limo and drove off. Hailing a cab back to my apartment, I nervously paced around the room, waiting for Drew to arrive. What if he didn't want me anymore? After all, he did bring another woman to my sister's wedding. The minute I heard the knock on the door, my heart started racing and the nervousness that I felt was at an all-time high. I stood there for a moment with my hand on the doorknob and took in a deep breath.

"Hi."

"Hi." Drew smiled as he stepped inside. "You wanted to talk?"

"Yeah." I began to pace around the living room.

"Do you want to sit down?" he asked.

"No. You sit. I'm just going to pace around. There are some things I need to say to you."

"Okay." He took a seat on the couch.

Taking in a deep long breath, I held it for a moment before letting it out.

"I want to apologize to you for being a bitch."

"You aren't a bitch, Jillian. Don't ever say that."

Turning around, I held up my finger. "Yes. Yes, I am. I led you on. Made you think that there was something more between us than just friends. I let you have sex with me, multiple times. We did things together that couples do and then when you mentioned the word 'us,' I freaked out. And you want to know why I freaked out? Because as much as I wanted to be alone and be on my own with no distractions, I liked 'us.' I liked having sex with you multiple times a day. I liked going shopping for dishes. I liked going out to eat with you and I liked waking up to you every morning. I liked how you held me at night and made me feel safe, and I liked how you understood me and wanted to take care of me."

"I liked all that too," he spoke.

"No. No. Don't speak yet until I'm finished."

A small smile crossed his lips.

"I was lost, so lost in a world where I didn't exactly know where I belonged. I was struggling to find myself and my place in this world. And then I met you, and suddenly, I didn't feel lost anymore. Which, by the way, scared me because it wasn't supposed to happen that way. When you left that night, I felt lost again and I hated the fact that I needed you so much in my life and not just as a friend. Now you've met someone else and, to be honest, I'm having a hard time handling it. There, I said it."

"Can I speak now?"

Taking in a deep breath, I spoke, "Yes."

Getting up from the couch, he walked over to me and placed a tight grip on my hips.

"Lia is my secretary. She's not someone I'm interested in. I only brought her to the wedding to make you jealous and I deeply apologize for that. I know I'm a dick and I hope you can forgive me."

"So, she's not someone you're dating?"

"No, Jill." He smiled. "She's my secretary and a damn good one. I'm not interested in dating anyone else. You're the only woman in this world I want. You had me in the palm of your hand the minute you sat down next to me on that plane. I can't explain it. I wish I could, but I can't. I have never felt this way about anyone before. I am so in love with you, Jillian Bell, that sometimes it hurts. You're all I think about every second of every day and you're all I dream about at night. I love you, you crazy girl, and I don't want to stop you from finding yourself, but I'll be there for you every step of the way. I promise."

Tears rolled down my cheeks as our eyes stayed locked on each other's and he took his thumbs and gently wiped them away.

"You're beautiful when you cry." He smiled.

"When I started my journey, nothing was getting in my way; there were no exceptions. Except you became the exception because I couldn't help but fall in love with you."

"Do you know how happy that makes me to hear you say that?" Tears filled his eyes. "I love you, Jillian."

"I love you too, Drew, and if you'll have me, I would like there to be an us."

"That's all I ever wanted, baby." His lips brushed against mine.

"Good lord!" I exclaimed as Drew rolled off me.

He chuckled as he sat up against the headboard and I snuggled into him.

"Satisfied?" he asked.

"Very." I moaned as my lips pressed against his chest. "You?"

"Very satisfied." He kissed the top of my head.

His fingers softly ran themselves up and down my arm as he held me.

"My dad is divorcing my mom," I spoke.

"I'm sorry, baby."

"Don't be. It's for the best." I sat up and ran my thumb across his lip. "I'm hungry."

"Want to grab a bite to eat somewhere?"

"Yeah." I smiled as I kissed his lips. "And then we can have dessert at your house."

Chapter Forty-One
Drew

After grabbing some dinner, we headed to my townhouse. As I was helping Jillian from the car, Liam and Oliver had just stepped out his front door.

"Hello there, neighbor!" Liam shouted as he waved.

Here we go.

"Hey, Liam. Oliver." I waved back.

"Hello, Jillian." Liam smiled.

"Hi, Liam." She waved.

They walked over to us and Liam introduced Jillian to Oliver.

"This is my brother, Oliver Wyatt."

"Nice to meet you, Oliver." She smiled as they shook hands.

"Nice to meet you as well, Jillian."

"Why don't you go in the house and put these leftovers in the refrigerator. I'll be in shortly," I spoke.

Jillian went into the house and I prepared myself for Liam.

Placing his hands in his pocket, he spoke, "So, what's going on?"

"Okay. Okay." I put up my hand. "It seems your little plan worked. We are officially a couple now." I grinned.

"Congratulations." Oliver placed his hand on my shoulder.

"Thanks."

"Yep. Told you it would work. I think I may start my own business," Liam spoke.

"And what business would that be?" Oliver asked as he rolled his eyes.

"A company that helps a man or a woman get the person of their dreams."

"You're an idiot." Oliver smacked him upside the head.

"Why? Something like, uh, what's it called, a wingman service. I could be the wingman and help people out in the love department." He grinned brightly.

I laughed and Oliver stood there shaking his head. "Like I said, you're an idiot."

"You say that now, but you won't be when I start raking in the millions, dear brother."

Oliver sighed. "You already rake in the millions. Come on, we're going to be late. Congrats, Drew. I'm happy for you, man."

"Yeah. Congratulations, bro. The six of us need to do dinner. Call me!" He pointed at me as they headed to the car.

"I will, and thanks again."

Liam held his arms out. "That's what a wingman does, bro."

Chuckling, I walked into the house and found Jillian in the kitchen, pouring us a glass of wine.

"I've been thinking," she spoke. "I'm going to take the bar exam."

"Really? I thought you didn't want to be a lawyer?" I asked as I wrapped my arms around her waist.

"I worked my ass off in college and law school and it would be waste at least not to take the exam."

"I think it's a good idea. I'll tell you what, you can come work for me as my company lawyer if you want to. I'd hire you on the spot."

"Don't you have a lawyer already?"

I shrugged. "A firm. But they can easily be replaced by someone as sexy as you." I smiled as I kissed her lips.

"We'd have to work together every day. We'd see each other all the time. Don't you think we'd get sick of each other?"

"I could never get sick of having you by my side all day long."

A smile graced her beautiful face. "Good, because I could never get sick of you either. There's something else I need to do."

"What's that, baby?"

"I need to go see Grant and my mom. It's part of my journey. For closure purposes."

"Do you want me to come with you?"

"Yes. If you wouldn't mind."

"I would be happy to go with you."

"Thank you. I love you."

"And I love you. Now about that dessert you promised me." I grinned as my hand traveled up her short skirt.

"Where would you like to eat it, Mr. Westbrook?" The corners of her mouth curved upwards.

"I was thinking right here in the kitchen." I lifted her up on the counter.

"The kitchen is the perfect place for dessert." Our lips met with passion.

****

Jillian

As Drew and I stepped off the plane, I thought I'd feel nervous, but I wasn't. Which was weird. When I turned on my phone, a message from Kellan came through.

"Douchebag is at Bar Louie and he's here with some chick. I'm sitting at the bar trying not to gag."

"Thanks. Did he see you?"

"Yeah. When he was on his way to the bathroom. He just gave me a dirty look. Idiot."

"We're on our way."

"You sure you want to do this, Bean?"

"I'm sure. See you soon."

"He's at Bar Louie with some girl," I spoke as I held Drew's hand.

"Don't you think you should wait and talk to him at his house?"

"And risk seeing his parents? Um. No thanks. A public place is better."

When we reached Bar Louie, I took in a deep breath as I walked through the door and saw Kellan sitting at the bar. Walking over, I gave him a big hug.

"So where is he?" I asked.

"Well, he's walking over to us as we speak. Shit. Are you sure about this?"

"Look who decided to pop back into town," Grant spoke as he approached me.

I swallowed hard. "Hello, Grant."

Drew took a seat on the stool and ordered a scotch.

"'Hello, Grant'? Is that all you have to say?"

"No. I have a lot to say. So how about we go over to that table and talk?"

"Nah. I have nothing to say to you, Jillian. Do you even realize the embarrassment you caused me and my family?" He grabbed hold of my arm.

"I suggest you let go of her right now," Drew spoke in anger.

"And you are?" Grant cocked his head.

"The person who's going to scar up that pretty little face of yours if you don't remove your hand from her."

"I'd like to see you try it, big man."

Drew stood up from his stool and I stepped in between him and Grant.

"Stop it. I didn't come here to argue. I came to talk to you. To put closure on us."

Grant let out a loud laugh. "Us? There never was any us, Jill. I was marrying you out of obligation. Do you know how many women I fucked behind your back over the years?"

I didn't think he could hurt me, but he did, and I needed to get over it real quick.

"Did you honestly believe I loved you? The only thing you were good for was a social status."

An anger ripped through me and my breathing became rapid. I couldn't control myself as I balled my hand into a fist and punched him, sending him down to the ground. I kneeled down and grabbed hold of his fucking polo shirt I hated so much.

"Do you know how long I've been wanting to do that, you little fuckwad?"

"Oh my God!" The girl he was with came running over.

"Get out of here or you're next!" I yelled at her. Looking back at Grant, who was lying there holding his jaw, I spoke, "Now I've embarrassed you twice. I came here to have a civil conversation to put closure on what happened, but no, you had to go run your smart mouth like you always do. The best thing I ever did was leave your dumb ass at the altar, and now I've said my peace. Have a nice life, Grant." I let go of his shirt and stood up. "Come on, Drew. Come on, Kellan. Let's get out of here." I turned on my heels and walked out the door.

"Shit, Jill. I didn't know you had that in you," Kellan spoke as he caught up with me.

"Are you okay?" Drew asked with concern.

"I've never felt better." I smiled.

Chapter Forty-Two
Jillian
One Year Later

I could hear the soft music play as the guests started to gather inside and took their seats in the luxurious chairs that were beautifully decorated with white satin bows and white roses. As I stared at myself in the full-length mirror, I recognized the girl staring back at me. Her name was Jillian Bell, soon to be Mrs. Jillian Westbrook. This was my wedding day and I couldn't have been happier.

So much had happened in the past year. Kellan moved to New York and got a job on Wall Street making twice as much as he was back in Seattle. I took my bar exam and passed with flying colors, landing me a job at Westbrook Technology. Kristen passed away six months ago. It was a difficult time for all of us, but she made us promise that we would only grieve for a short time and move on with our lives and live life to the fullest. She made Noah promise that he'd find someone to love as much as he loved her. As heartbroken as I was not to have my sister standing by my side at my wedding, I knew she was watching over me. My dad visited New York frequently and him and Kristen became close as a father and daughter should be. I tried to reconnect with my mother, but there was only so much effort I could put in. We talked occasionally and she refused to come to my wedding, but that was her problem, not mine. I forgave her, though, because I wasn't going to let her cast a shadow over my life anymore.

A nervousness rose up inside me as a thought crossed my mind. Running to the door of the suite I was in, I opened it.

"Jill, where are you going?" Kellan asked.

"I'll be right back," I said as I flew out into the hallway.

I stopped when I saw Drew standing there, staring at me. I bit down on my bottom lip as a smile crossed my face.

"What are you doing?" I asked.

"I was coming to make sure you weren't going to bail on me," he spoke with a smile. "What are you doing?"

"I was just coming to make sure you weren't going to bail on me."

He walked over to where I was standing and grabbed my hands, holding them tight.

"My God, you are so beautiful."

"So are you."

"I'll see you at the end of the aisle." He brought my hand up to his lips.

"I'll see you there."

Drew and I were married under an opulent canopy in the Grand Ballroom of the Plaza Hotel, following a beautiful reception that consisted of over four hundred guests. It was time to take our first dance as husband and wife to Ed Sheeran's song

"Thinking Out Loud." Placing my hand in his, we walked out onto the dance floor.

"Do you know how happy you've made me?" Drew asked.

"I hope as happy as you've made me."

My heart melted as he leaned his lips close to my ear and began singing to me.

"And, darling, I will be loving you till we're seventy. And, baby, my heart could still fall as hard at twenty-three."

"You're making me cry." I looked up at him with a tear in my eye.

"Oh, baby, we found love right where we are." He smiled.

After the reception was coming close to an end, Drew and I headed to the yacht he rented for us for a two-week honeymoon. A honeymoon that consisted of the open water and just the two of us.

"I can't wait to get you out of this dress and make love to you all night long, Mrs. Westbrook," he spoke as he carried me onto the yacht.

"This will be the first time we have sex as a married couple. Do you think you can handle it? I may get a little rough." I smirked.

"I can handle it just fine. The question is will you be able to handle it?" he spoke as he laid me down on the bed.

"I guess we'll find out. Your performance has to top all the others over the past year. Are you up to the challenge?" I smiled.

"Oh, I can promise you that my performance will outdo anything you've ever experienced." He growled as his mouth smashed into mine. "I love you, Jillian."

"And I love you, Drew."

About The Author

Sandi Lynn is a New York Times, USA Today and Wall Street Journal bestselling author who spends all of her days writing. She published her first novel, Forever Black, in February 2013 and hasn't stopped writing since. Her addictions are shopping, going to the gym, romance novels, coffee, chocolate, margaritas, and giving readers an escape to another world.

Please come connect with her at:

www.facebook.com/Sandi.Lynn.Author

www.twitter.com/SandilynnWriter

www.authorsandilynn.com

www.pinterest.com/sandilynnWriter

www.instagram.com/sandilynnauthor

https://www.goodreads.com/author/show/6089757.Sandi_Lynn

Printed in Great Britain
by Amazon